GREG'S
REVENGE

George Hendry

Blackie

GREG'S
REVENGE

Copyright © 1991 George Hendry
First published 1991 by Blackie and Son Ltd

A CIP catalogue record for this book is
available from the British Library.

ISBN 0 216 93201 7

Blackie and Son Ltd
7 Leicester Place
London WC2H 7BP

Printed in Great Britain by
Thomson Litho Ltd, East Kilbride, Scotland

Chapter One

A long, smooth wave gathered towards the shore. Two stones splashed into it, one slightly ahead of the other.

'Beat you by miles.'

'No, you didn't, you cheated. Moved your foot. I saw you. You must think I'm blind, Hacker.'

'I just think you can't take being beaten.'

'I wasn't beaten. I threw from the line and you took an extra step.'

The wave reached land, broke on the shingle and rushed up to where the boys still argued. It took them by surprise and foamed over their shoes with a surge and a drag of pebbles. Ice cold.

'Your fault we're soaked!' shouted the first boy. 'Standing there giving lectures.'

'Your fault for needing someone to tell you the rules,' said the other.

Competitions for throwing pebbles into the sea always led to arguments. The movement of the waves made it difficult to judge distance, no two pebbles are ever exactly the same size and Greg Blake knew that his best friend, Bill Yates – 'Hacker' Yates to everyone because of the way he played football – was notorious for stealing at least one step as he threw. He would even take a short run if he thought he could get away with it.

But the sea can alter more than a pair of shoes.

'It's a good job,' his father had said, standing in the kitchen with a letter in his hand; a letter headed in blue lettering with flags and a crest; a letter from a shipping company.

His mother was delighted. She'd read it and given Greg's father a kiss. 'Fantastic!' she'd said.

'Bit far though,' replied his father. 'You don't mind, do you? Be a bit of a trek moving up there.'

'Nothing to it,' she said. 'We've moved before. It'll be all right. I know it will.'

Greg lived in Eastbourne. Neat and tidy Eastbourne. He liked it. He enjoyed being close to the sea. The sea was important. His father earned his living in the merchant navy and Eastbourne was not a difficult journey from Southampton which was where he usually joined ship. Joined, that is, before he was made redundant. The line he worked for sold out to a larger company and not everyone was required by the new owners. 'Turned me out like an old horse being put to grass.' His father had spoken both in hurt and anger.

For some months nothing happened. He applied for jobs but got nowhere, not even a first interview. Then things changed, suddenly his luck was in.

Alan Blake got a job in Scotland as master of an oil rig supply boat sailing out of the small and pretty east coast port of Montrose, just South of Aberdeen. He would work throughout the year, two weeks on and two weeks off, taking supplies to the drilling rigs. All sorts of things were shipped out but especially lengths of piping for the drills themselves and a specialised kind of mud made from the dense rock, Pyrites. The Pyrites mud is pumped down the pipes to the drill head to keep it cool and to act as a plug in case gas or oil tries to blow back.

On the last night he spent in Eastbourne, Greg lay

awake for a long time wondering what Scotland would be like.

It proved impossible to find a house near Montrose; prices had gone sky high because of the oil and by the time Alan Blake's job had come along there was, in any case, very little left on the market. This initial disappointment turned eventually to their advantage because the Blakes moved inland, miles inland, almost as near to the middle of Scotland as it is possible for a merchant seaman from Eastbourne to reach. And there they found a house for sale. They took one look and bought it.

For the first night in the new house Greg slept on the floor, lying on a mattress surrounded by packing cases and bundles of various shapes and sizes, all of which meant something to his mother and nothing to him. There were, as yet, no curtains and he slept with the window slightly open. It was the end of April. The unoccupied house smelled stale when they first moved in but the outside air was already laced with the scent of new grass and he fell asleep with this cool sweetness drifting into his room.

It was a stone-built house, quite unlike the bricks and coloured facings of Eastbourne. The walls were a mosaic of grey stones of different shapes and sizes with silver flecks of mica twinkling out of them in the sunlight. Here and there were streaks and patches of white quartz as if snow balls, flung against the walls, had stayed there for ever. In the walls he even found clusters of garnets; dark ruby gemstones, semi-precious if cut and polished, some as big as the nail on a little finger but all too coarse and poorly formed to be worth anything. But their lack of value did not diminish the enthusiasm with which Greg chipped some of them out of their hard beds using a hammer and an old screwdriver. He soon had enough to fill a match box. 'I've heard of the streets being paved with gold,' said his father, 'But this is a laugh. Fancy living in a house with gemstones in the walls!'

Greg had taken the garnets upstairs to his room and laid the match box on the cream-painted mantelpiece. He felt as if the stones had welcomed him to their domain and often he would take them out of their box and hold them cool and heavy in the palm of his hand.

However, the first actual discovery concerning the garnet house was of a different nature. He awoke early on his first morning; half past five. Already it was light enough to make out the gaunt surroundings of his unpacked room. It wasn't the light that had woken him but a sound.

Most of the house was surrounded by flower-beds, then by a wide sweep of gravel which led to the front gate. All his attention now concentrated on the gravel. He heard the small stones, or rather he heard something moving as if on tiptoe across them, right up to the house, stopping, it seemed, directly under his window. He got up and at once felt cold and vulnerable in the morning air. Crouching down, he edged on bare feet towards the window and, as carefully as possible, trying not to reveal his presence, he looked out. Greg gave a quiet gasp.

There were four of them; a buck with wide, flat antlers and three hinds or rather, two hinds and a last year's calf. The intruders were fallow deer. He recognized them from a trip he and his mother had made to the New Forest on one occasion when they had driven down to Southampton to meet his father. The deer were eating lobelia from the flower-beds, browsing the lawn and threatening clusters of late daffodils, although they seemed indifferent to whatever taste these had and left them alone. In summer, Greg was to discover their taste for roses, a craving which would bring them, fearless, up to the house, until his father admitted defeat and had a proper deer fence put around the house and garden. Greg never got used to having fallow coming in so close, it thrilled him equally each and every time, but this morning, being the first, he gazed in astonishment and joy.

Greg watched for what seemed an eternity although it couldn't have been more than two minutes. They moved away from the house and back over the gravel towards a strip of lawn. Again he heard the delicate, crisp sound of hooves on pebbles. This time Dusty must have heard it too, downstairs in the kitchen, or perhaps he got a scent of them with all the other new scents that the previous twenty-four hours had brought him. Greg heard the dog stir. 'Quiet, Dusty,' he said to himself. 'Quiet or you'll frighten them off!' But Dusty let out a parent-waking bark and in the twinkling of an eye the deer were tails up and in full flight, taking the fence between garden and neighbouring field with a graceful contempt. He watched them pick up rhythm across the field, short strides quickly becoming long, easy, gliding bounds. In no time they had crossed the field and disappeared into the woods beyond.

Downstairs, the dog was full of his own importance, still barking and snuffling at the door to be let out. The sound of his paws on the uncovered floor rang in the hall along with his barking. Although his parents must have been wakened by now Greg ran to the door and let the dog out. Dusty rushed about, gulping in the fresh scent of the intruders and letting off a last bark or two.

'Greg? What's all the rumpus? Why have you let the dog out?' It was his father, half-way down the stairs.

9

'Deer,' hissed Greg, as if they were still outside. 'Four of them, right under my window.'

'Never.'

'Honest. There were. Dusty must have heard them. He's put them off. I had to let him out. He's in such a state.'

'So I can hear. Call him in before he wakes the whole place and then you'd better get back to bed.' His father returned upstairs.

In pyjamas, Greg stood against the doorpost and called to Dusty. From the front door he could almost see down to the village. Already smoke was rising from some of the chimneys. When the dog grew silent, it was so quiet that he could hear the sound of the river that divided the village. All around were hills, trees of every kind, each in new leaf and between the hills and trees, green spaces. Everything was clothed in a greenery so pure that he couldn't believe his eyes. Greg murmured to it all, 'I'm going to like it here. Oh, yes. I'm going to like it.'

It was a Tuesday when the Blakes arrived in their new house. With so much in the way of change going on, his parents decided that Greg could have a few days settling in before starting at the village school on the following Monday. Nothing could have suited him better.

He did what he could to help with the unpacking but succeeded only in getting in the way. His parents had moved several times before and knew their way around the harassing art of packing and unpacking. Both were neat and tidy, good with their hands. His father turned carpenter, carpet-fitter or general handyman with equal ease, and at a table in the large kitchen his mother produced a sewing-machine and started running up new curtains and altering old as if there were no tomorrow.

There was, however, one difference with this move. In the past, packing-cases and cardboard boxes had been folded flat where possible and everything stored away for future use; this time they only got as far as a bonfire in the garden.

'Here, Greg. Job for you,' said his father. 'See that nothing lifts off this fire and sets the place up.' Greg stood by the fire with a long pole and made sure that nothing blew away.

Starting with the village, Greg, with Dusty in tow, took to exploring. It was an old place with low squat houses and a market square. There was a steep road down from where the new house and a few others sat on a hillside, but he quickly discovered a little path which led down by a back way, opening out onto a steep street that led down into the market square.

The village was divided in two by a river, a wide river crossed by an old stone bridge. On the other side from where Greg lived was the school, a church and a newer part of the village. The square was pretty with all the usual shops plus a lot selling things for tourists. The bridge impressed him more than the square.

It was a long stone-built bridge with four arches. On it Greg discovered a fascination for running water. To start with, the noise of water rushing past the base of the arches reminded him briefly of the sea, although the pattern of sound was quite different. Except where the light shone off it, or where the current churned up cascades of froth or forced it into glassy, sleek, black curves, the water was clear.

There were many places where Greg could see the beds of gravel on the bottom, with strands of weed which at first he mistook for fish. Down-stream from the bridge was a small island with a narrow beach of white stones

11

washed smooth and round. Behind this little beach stood scrubby trees; birch and alder, some Scots pine and along the water's edge, the bright and spindly red and yellow branches of willow.

For half an hour Greg looked over the bridge and watched the river; already *his* river, never growing tired of it, noticing perhaps even more than the locals, unless they were the fishing kind, just how much it changed. Not for two moments did it stay the same. It altered with every flicker of light and wind, with every bird or cloud of insects that moved across it.

On the far side of the bridge there was a track which ran along the river-bank down to the church and the school. It looked as if it might be a tempting short cut in the mornings.

After a few days Greg had been up and down both sides of the river, over most of the fields and low ground and had covered and covered again the wood nearest to where he lived. It was a great bank of young oak and the ground beneath the trees was a carpet of blaeberries.

Then there were the hills to climb. Greg couldn't do everything at once but the hill behind his house begged to be conquered. One morning he rushed up it with Dusty panting alongside. He soon learnt that he saw much more if he took his time, but the view from the top justified his hurry. A wide valley or strath swept north towards more hills and the next town; below him lay his house, looking like a toy thing, and the village spread out like a map.

Chapter Two

His first Monday in the new village came round and Greg started school. His father had gone through to his ship the day before, so Greg was signed on by his mother.

His mother tended to fuss on such occasions and was over-anxious to please and make a good impression. This only led to mistakes, of which, on this particular Monday, Mrs Blake made two. To start with and in spite of his protests, Greg was made to turn out in the uniform of his previous school, which was bound to make him stick out like a sore thumb when all he wanted to do was to be as inconspicuous as possible. But the embarrassment of wearing an odd uniform became a disaster when he discovered that he was the only one with a uniform at all. The school playground, when he and his mother arrived, was full of milling children wearing everyday clothes, anything and everything. Greg could have died.

'Mum, didn't you ask if there was a uniform? Everybody's staring, I can't spend the day like this.'

'No, I didn't ask. And, yes, you can and will spend the day as you are. I've never heard of a school without a uniform. You don't ask about something you take for granted. Stop being so silly about something trivial.'

Trivial? thought Greg. The thing was massive.

Being embarrassed makes you tense, being tense affects the way you walk. Walking towards the school door with his mother, Greg moved like a robot. Matters were made worse by his mother's second mistake. He was wearing new shoes, squeaky clean and brand-new that morning. It was more calamitous than wearing new boots at a cup-tie. They were heavy, uncomfortable, awkward and most important, worse than anything, entirely representative of how he felt.

As they approached the school door, a large man wearing a baggy navy-blue boiler suit and a peaked bus-driver hat opened the door and waddled down the few steps. Two paces from the steps was a long rope hanging down the wall, encased for most of its length inside a black metal pipe to protect it from the weather.

'There's the janny,' someone said, and a second later the school bell swung into action as the janitor pulled on the rope. It hardly took two minutes for the door to syphon the school yard empty. Inside the door, Greg and his mother found themselves in a crowded corridor being steered by a human tide towards the gym where morning assembly was held.

It took to that point for Greg's mother to realise that she had made a mistake, a real mistake, something over and above the complaints concerning uniform and shoes. They were half an hour early. She was supposed to appear at the headmasters' office at nine-thirty, after assembly, when the day was safely started. Now it was her turn to feel embarrassed. She turned to Greg and was about to speak.

'I know,' he said. 'You don't have to tell me. This is no time for a quiet introductory chat with the head. We're early, Mum. You should have checked his letter. I bet it said half-past nine. God, I feel like a right plinth.'

A 'plinth' had been his Eastbourne slang for the ultimate in feeling embarrassed and at that moment he took refuge in travelling back to the south coast, to be with his old mates, to tell Hacker Yates – and anybody else

14

who'd listen – about his mother's mismanagement, which had gone so contrary to all his instincts about starting at a new school. Mentally he unburdened himself and heard the comfort of familiar voices.

'Blimey, son, bet you felt like a plinth. Mothers have no idea. No sense of your feelings,' said Hecker.

'It is unpleasing to be plinthed by the mother.' It was Eddie Smith. Quiet Eddie with specs who liked to have the last word and speak slightly differently from everyone else. He should know. His mother once pressed his jeans.

Greg's flight back to Eastbourne was interrupted by the sight of a tall white-headed man in black academic gown coming to meet them down the corridor, the crowd somehow finding space to make way for him. He billowed up to Greg and his mother, extending his hand to her.

'You must be Mrs Blake. I'm David McDonald, headmaster. You're good and early, keen to make a start, eh? And this must be Gregory. Pleased to meet you Gregory and welcome to Kirkbrae.'

David McDonald had turned towards Greg and they shook hands. Greg immediately noticed two things about this new headmaster: he pronounced the letter 'r' like gravel going under a road roller and his handshake was hydraulic.

'I'm sorry we're a bit early,' began Greg's mother. 'Your letter did say nine-thirty, only I got it into my head as nine o'clock.'

'No matter,' said McDonald. 'Come and join assembly. We can have a chat afterwards in my office.'

Greg and his mother found seats at the rear of the gym and listened into assembly, which consisted that Monday of a mixture of prayers, football results, time-table adjustments, a forthcoming talk on astronomy by a local expert for those interested, news that some pupil had been involved in a road accident and would all of his class please write to him and the last warning that any lost property not collected by the end of the week would this time definitely be burned.

Throughout assembly, furtive backwards glances had been taken in Greg's direction and now, horror of horrors, he was introduced by the head so that everyone had official permission to turn and take a look. Greg stared hard at the narrow pine floorboards and prayed that they might open and swallow him up. But they didn't.

The meeting Greg and his mother had in the head's office was brief. The curriculum was broadly the same as in his last school, and such differences as existed were not likely to cause Greg much trouble. He was a boy who learned quickly when he wanted to, but could, according to every school report he'd ever brought home, have done better if he wasn't such a dreamer.

To start with his mother had nagged him about the day-dreaming tag but his father knew better and put her mind at ease. He'd been at sea long enough to have met at close quarters all kinds of men. He knew that everyone is a dreamer somewhere, sometime, in their heart of hearts and that they all tasted the world differently. Some, more than others needed to mull things over in their minds before they felt comfortable with new facts. Knowledge to them is very personal, they have to make it fit like friendly old clothes. Alan Blake had always known that was how it was with Greg.

In the corridor outside his office, David McDonald and Greg's mother said goodbye to each other. Clutching a history of the school and lists of governors, societies, clubs and PTA meetings, she made her way down the passage towards the door by the bell-rope. As the sharp clack of her heels receded, Greg's confidence grew. Of course, she had to come along this morning, but mothers can cramp your style and he felt more relaxed once she had gone.

There would be, he knew, one more mass introduction. The head took him along to his class where together with his teacher, a neat and pretty Mrs Thompson, he stood stoically in front of the class and died the death as 'Gregory from Eastbourne' was introduced. Then it was over, the head left, he was issued with enough books to start the week, told his teacher what maths he'd been doing, since Mondays started with maths, and found his way to a desk.

Mrs Thompson had enough sense to indulge the curiosity which any class feels over a new arrival and asked them all if they knew where Eastbourne was.

'Doon in England, miss,' was the reply but when a map of southern Britain was chalked on the board there were only one or two who put it within driving distance of Brighton. When Greg thought of the two days it had taken him and his parents to drive up, the 'Doon in England' location made him laugh.

A wiry little boy called Alistair, all red hair and freckles, was detailed to look after Greg on his first day, to show him around and to see that he wasn't left out. It was a kind thought on the part of his teacher and Alistair took his role seriously, giving Greg more information per hour than he either required or could remember. A running commentary continued throughout the day, a who's who of the school and district, who was related to whom, where they all lived, who was all right and who was a pain.

From maths, Monday moved to woodwork where Greg was quickly issued with enough wood to make a four-legged stool. He had his fathers' ability in making things and he was grateful for the chance to get his hands on some tools. Planing and squaring up helped work off the tension of the first day.

The same goes for sport and here Greg had a piece of luck. The day ended with a gym session which turned into an indoor football match, five-a-side. Greg quite liked football, no more than quite liked it and had never considered himself much good, but for some reason on that particular Monday everything came his way and he couldn't put a foot wrong. Five-a-side moves fast and in no time he'd scored a hat-trick. It had never happened before and he didn't expect it ever to happen again but naturally he'd enough sense to keep that thought to himself. The others, of course, believed that this was his normal game and were suitably impressed, especially Alistair whose loyalty deepened by the minute.

'Ye didnae say ye were guid wi the baw.'

'I'm not anything special,' said Greg.

'Well ye'r no ordinary either,' was the reply.

Alistair lived on Greg's side of the river and after school they walked home together across the bridge, where they stopped and looked over. Greg's new guide pointed out a 'lie o' troot', a shingle bed where half a dozen large trout were almost always to be seen, lying in a sheltered piece of water which the current kept well supplied with food. It surprised Greg that he hadn't noticed those fish before and from then on there was hardly a time he would cross that bridge and not look for them.

The two boys parted half-way along the short High Street where Alistair cut left down into the square and Greg turned right up the steep little street which led to the pathway for home. It had been a long day. He enjoyed the familiarity of the path; its cool shade where hazel and elderberry overhung from disused terraced gardens.

Dusty sensed it had been a big day and gave him a

18

tumultuous welcome, rushing inside as he always did to fetch a cushion or a piece of wood in a frenzy of joy and showing-off, tail wagging fit to clear a coffee table.

'How was your first day, love?' asked his mother from the top of a step-ladder from which she was painting a ceiling.

'All right,' said Greg. 'Mum, do you want a joke?' Without waiting for a reply he continued, 'Do you know what I am?'

'What's that then?'

'Guid wi' the baw.'

'You're what?'

'I'm good at football, or so everybody thinks just because I had a good game today.'

'That's nice, love, but I always thought you couldn't play your way out of a paper bag.'

Greg's face fell. 'Well, here it's different. Although God knows how I'll keep it up.'

'Course you can,' said his mother. 'And Dusty thinks you can, don't you, Dusty?' And the dog spun and fussed as if Greg had made the World Cup squad.

One Friday morning, six weeks after starting at Kirkbrae, Greg was late for school. He'd left home in good enough time but spent too long trying to reach a bird's nest high up in the dry-stone wall that held up part of the terraced gardens on the path he took to the village. In the end he succeeded in peering into the nest and onto a clutch of four song-thrush eggs, each the purest azure blue speckled with small black dots and all safely gathered into the middle of the mud-lined nest. It was a late clutch, too early for a proper second brood so the birds must have lost their original eggs to magpies or crows or schoolboys – or perhaps cats or pine-martens had taken the chicks.

By the time Greg reached the pathway on the school side of the bridge he was going at a steady trot, holding his schoolbag under his arm like a rugby ball. He was breathing quite hard. There was the noise of the river, of his feet beating on the hard track, of something metallic rattling to his footsteps from inside the bag, but over and above it all, a shrill and urgent piping from down by the river-bank. A cry of distress, no doubting that, whatever was making it.

Greg stopped running and stood still, aware that he ought definitely to be carrying on. It came again, the peal of squeaking and this time he placed it down by some alder growing tall by the bank. Laying his bag in the grass by the side of the path, he slipped down under the branches. The trees grew some little way in from the waters' edge but leant and spread out above the river, throwing a green tunnel over the strip of shingle on which Greg knelt. About ten feet out from the bank Greg saw the source of all the noise.

It's not unusual for fishermen to lose hooks and nylon casts on riverside trees and hanging from this alder was a tangle of nylon and a cast of four flies which dangled into the water. Caught on one of those flies was a duckling, a young mallard, a bundle of black and yellow fluff no more than three days out of the egg and every few minutes squeaking fit to burst.

It would run along the surface of the water on frantic feet, squeaking as the line went slack then, the moment it stopped, it was swept back downstream until the line pulled it tight again. To start with Greg thought that it had swallowed one of the hooks, but on looking closer, he saw that the hook was caught through one of those two holes in a duck's beak that pass for nostrils.

Greg's first thought was to wade out and disentangle

the duckling, but even at that distance the water was waist deep and too strong to stand against. He would have to bring it closer to the shore, but the line was well out of reach and there was no way that the overhead limbs would bear his weight. Nor did he have any success in breaking off a green branch with which he might have caught the line and pulled it within reach. The more he pulled and twisted at the Alder, the more it bent and frayed and refused to break. He swore never again to be without a penknife.

The duck kept up such a volume of noise that Greg decided it couldn't have been caught for too long and almost certainly couldn't have been there overnight. If it were quite out of luck then a large pike might take it, but that was a risk it would have to run. Greg left the bank and went looking for something with which to hook the line and bring it in close enough for him to reach.

Twenty yards downstream and long after the school bell had gone quiet, Greg found an old piece of wire fence, fallen down and overgrown in the tall grass. He broke off a piece of wire about eight feet long by bending it backwards and forwards quickly until it grew almost too hot to hold and snapped. Armed with this wire, now bent over at one end to make a crook, he hurried back to where he'd left the duckling. It was still there.

The way the current took the line away from the bank still made it difficult to reach, so Greg took off his shoes, socks and trousers and waded out up to his knees, feeling anything but secure as the ice-cold water forced against him.

It was now or never, he couldn't stand there all morning. Gingerly, he stretched out his home-made line-catcher and hooked it onto the nylon cast, twisting it round once or twice before pulling it and the now frantic duckling towards him.

As he drew his catch in the light branches that held the nylon bent over so much that Greg had a sudden horror of a few critical twigs snapping off and the line plus duckling floating off downstream. When he had the line as near to himself as the wire would bring it, the duckling still had enough cast to allow it to stay out of Greg's reach so he took the cast carefully in both hands, tucking the wire under his arm and pulled the fluff ball in. The duckling was hooked, as he had suspected, through one of the holes in its beak, but was otherwise unharmed. It kicked and struggled in his gentle grasp and scratched the palm of his hand.

Once the duckling was disengaged from the flyhook, Greg debated what to do with it. If he took it to school it would explain why he was late, or he might take it home and rear it as a pet; it would take some looking after, but he could talk his mother round and manage somehow. Then he thought of leaving it on the river-bank but something told him not to. In the end the duckling decided for itself by wriggling quickly out of Greg's hand and back into the water where, in a split second, it was out of his reach and off downstream.

'Oh well,' thought Greg. 'Have things your own way. No doubt your mother and the rest of you are downstream somewhere. I hope so anyway.'

Greg pulled what he could of the line from the tree, rolled it into a ball and put it into his pocket before stumbling on blue-cold feet to the bank. Although he had retrieved the cast in order to prevent such a freak accident happening again, it had the added advantage of providing evidence to support his story. As it happened, the story was so fantastic that Mrs Thompson, although her mood was sharp that morning, would probably have believed him in any case.

But it was a strange day. Something was up, Greg felt it in his bones, felt it for sure. In school his powers of concentration were non-existent. That afternoon he sat with only half his mind on the lesson. The other half was directed partly towards the river and the duckling and partly outside where a May wind blew warm air up from the Azores and moved quickly-changing clouds across a blue sky. In a real sense it was the lesson to blame for his inattention. They had been looking at a map of the United States, at some of the rivers, rivers with magic in their names: Ohio, Missouri, Shenendoah, Arkansas and, largest of them all, the Mississippi.

The picture in his geography book showed a long string of barges full of hard durum wheat from the prairies going to be milled in New Orleans and made into pasta. Enough pasta, it seemed, to cover the school or fill the village streets. And moving upstream, being towed in the opposite direction, mountains of sugar from Guatemala for the refineries at St Louis. Then up in the Pacific North West there was the Colorado, flowing so strongly from where it rose miles and miles away almost in Canada that when in flood, the river could push fresh water three miles into the ocean. The thought of that kind of natural power and the distance echoing in these names caused Greg's mind to wander.

How else could anyone take it in except by looking up at the sky and imagining being able to fly straight out the window and soar away west so that they could actually see for themselves? No, it wasn't all his fault, some facts have to be savoured, thought about, lingered over.

'Greg! Gregory Blake! What have I just said? What have I just told you?'

'That Arkansas is pronounced Arkansaw, miss.'

23

'That was ten minutes ago. Where have you been?' His teacher paused. Perhaps she was reassessing his morning's story. 'Today, after school, I'll thank you to take a half-hour's detention and since your mind seems to have stopped at Arkansas, you can read the chapter summary on the Midwest and tell me about it first thing on Monday.'

'Yes, miss.' He wasn't as dismal as his voice suggested. The chapter would have to be read sometime by everyone and with his quick eye it wouldn't take half an hour.

There were about thirty others in his class, slightly more girls than boys, and he had never before noticed how much noise they all made as they left. The crashing and banging of chairs and desks, scuffling feet, schoolbags dragged along the floor, excited pent-up messages called out and, this afternoon, laughter and a few jokes at the expense of his predicament. He felt marooned.

Sue McCauley sat next to him. Every afternoon, as school broke up, she went through the ritual of packing a vast selection of pens and pencils into one of those pencil-cases made entirely from wood, one oblong block cut in half, longways, with top and bottom hollowed out to reveal almost secret chambers for the contents. The two halves swivelled open and shut on a screw at one end and then the top, which was also a ruler, slid into place. The case itself delighted him, but Greg also liked it because the ceremony of packing it away, which he witnessed every afternoon, signalled the end of school. But not today. Sue smiled, 'See you, dreamboat.'

Last to leave was Mrs Thomson. She paused and turned towards him by the door, holding in one arm a stack of work folders for correction. 'Half an hour means thirty minutes. And Mr Clark will tell me if you slip off early.'

Greg had no doubt as to the validity of this check on him. Mr Stanley Clark, the school janitor, had been known to generations as 'Sneaky Stan' and he would time him to the minute.

Suddenly his classmates were gone, no more than echoes. The school emptied quickly, even the last stragglers soon left the gate and he was becalmed in a hushed and strangely hollow-sounding room filled with that odour of bodies, chalk, paper, desks and dust that fills all classrooms.

The cleaners had arrived. He heard the clatter of a metal bucket and in the corridor outside he knew that Sneaky Stan would have already scattered that strange, damp, chemical-filled sand he put down to settle the dirt and dust. Shortly, with a wide, soft brush he would sweep the passageways, whispering the day with a slow rhythm into little heaps.

It felt odd to leave school alone. Apart from one of the cleaning ladies he saw no one and outside, the empty playground and deserted school gate felt peculiar. Normally the place was a mass of children, with groups hanging about waiting for the buses which drove home those who did not actually live in the village.

It was a rural community and all the children were country kids, but the ones who were bussed in were 'deep country', living mostly on farms anything up to fifteen miles away, some of them very isolated, with days off school in the winter weather. Between the village kids and the 'Strath' kids, that is those from further up the valley, there existed a rivalry which often led to scraps when school came out. The village kids considered themselves to be smarter than these 'teuchters' or peasants, which was unfortunate, because the Strath kids always seemed to do better academically. It was a painful truth for the village that most of the school prizes were bussed home at the end of the summer term.

25

Greg hurried past the black-painted cast-iron gate and headed for home, knowing that his mother was bound to ask why he was late and that he'd once again catch the edge of her tongue for being a dreamer. There had to be a moment of course, for stopping by the river-bank and having a quick look around for the duckling. Naturally, there was no sign of it but he reckoned that the chances of it rejoining the brood downstream had been good. From the river-bank he hurried up the stone steps which led to the bridge and pressed on home, thinking of how best to blame a geography lesson for the present situation. Try though he might, nothing plausible came to mind.

As he approached the end of the bridge a van drove towards him, a very old Ford Transit. It was white, but a battered white that showed the rust. The nearside wing was different from the rest of the body; clearly it had been bashed past redemption at some time and been replaced by a wing from a scrapped Transit; the other van had been dark blue. Perhaps it was the twin colour scheme that caught Greg's attention or perhaps he just happened to look up as the van drew close. In the passing vehicle, a few feet from where he stopped, was a girl of roughly his own age. She was the most beautiful girl he had ever seen. The most beautiful girl in the world. He knew that for certain. He stopped and stared, stopped wide-eyed in mid-stride while the moving van seemed for a moment to stop too and the girl looked at him. The van passed by taking the bridge slowly. Without being aware that he moved, Greg turned round as it passed and stared after it until it made the top of the bridge and disappeared from view.

'Why are you late?' asked his mother. 'Dad and me wondered if you hadn't got lost.'

'I missed a bit in geography and had to stay behind.'

'You mean, you were asked a question and hadn't been paying enough attention to answer?' His father was cleaning oil off his hands on a piece of cloth dipped in white spirit and spoke in a knowing voice. 'Just as well that changing the oil isn't a four-handed job or I might have waited long enough for some help.'

'Oh, Greg,' sighed his mother, 'You really must pay more attention. You're too old for all this dreaming and looking out of windows. School starts to become more serious at your age. We keep telling you.'

Dusty was in the middle of his gyrating welcome and the obligation to pay him some attention provided Greg with an excuse to avoid some of his mother's annoyance.

'Anything else in the way of excitement today?' asked his father. Greg stood there in the hall and told them about the duckling, a blow by blow account ending with the fly cast being produced from his pocket. This time his parents were more approving.

'And I saw an old van taking the bridge incredibly slowly, just creeping over it.' Greg stopped in horror and amazement. Why had he mentioned the van? It couldn't interest anyone else in the slightest. Why had he blurted out something so private, so precious? He must be going mad.

'A van on the bridge. What was so special about that?' His mother had asked the question he wished might not come.

'Nothing. Just that it was moving so slowly. I thought that it wasn't going to make it.'

'Exciting stuff,' said his father, giving his wife a quizzical look.

'Well, I thought so,' said Greg trying to sound convincing as he headed upstairs to change from his school clothes and collect what were left of his wits.

27

Chapter Three

It's all very well to say that animals know nothing apart from instinct and that they don't have a thought in their heads; the fact is that they do have their share of intelligence and that some of them have more than others. Although there was never any evidence to suggest that Dusty could count up to five or that he knew Saturday was the sixth day of the week, somehow, he always knew when Saturday came round. Perhaps he could tell a weekday by the normal routine of Greg getting ready for school and having to leave the house by a certain time which would have made Saturday easy to spot because then the routine changed. But however he worked it out, it wasn't that way, because long before the house thought of stirring, long before the normal hour of waking, the dog knew what day of the week it was and went into a routine of his own, specially reserved only for Saturday morning.

It was Greg's custom to take him out for a short walk before leaving for school, but on a Saturday the quick jaunt became at least a two hour ramble and for the start of this, Dusty could never wait.

He was a black Labrador, who had discovered that the door to Greg's room would always be opened if he threw his weight against it. On Saturday mornings early, six o'clock early, he would shoulder his way into Greg's room and make for the bed. The sleeper was usually woken up by having his face licked or an ear chewed. Sometimes his feet would receive the same treatment, or the dog would simply stick his great head under the duvet and snuffle about until he was noticed. Once or twice, when Dusty was still a pup, Greg had smuggled him into his bed for the night but now he was too large for such luxuries.

At three years, Dusty was in his prime, a shade high on the shoulder for the breed but a strong and willing dog. Around his neck hung a narrow leather collar with an identity disc worn into an oval shape through rubbing against the collar buckle. If you tickled him under this collar and along up to his ears he was your friend for life. He would stand perfectly still with his neck out stiff and moan with pleasure. He would react in the same way if you brushed him, which Greg did once a week out on the lawn, with cast hair drifting onto the grass and the dog in a seventh heaven. At the last brushing sparrows flew down from the roof top and snatched some dog hair for their nest-building under the eaves.

After his room had been invaded, Greg knew that it was futile to think of lying long in bed. Dusty would pace about in the house, rush up and down the stairs, whine at the front door to be let out and in no time whine again to be let back in. Feeding him breakfast caused some delay but he ate that in seconds flat and immediately resumed pressure for the off. By seven o'clock Greg had given in and after a quick breakfast and a rummage for a few biscuits to put in his pocket he set out, with the dog by now in a state of triumphant excitement.

It was a perfect May morning, fresh and bright. Hawthorn veiled a nearby hedge with hazy white flowers and the deep yellow of celandine shone out from the tall, dew-heavy grass by the gate.

Sometimes Greg would take his bike for a few miles if he felt like a change of ground and bring the dog alongside with a length of string attached to his collar. He was lean and fit, without that stockiness which creeps up easily on a home-kept Labrador. On these cycling mornings, Greg would eventually hide his bike at a spot he fancied and explore the new territory. Today, however, he was happy to walk on familiar ground and a few hundred yards from the house, he turned right and headed uphill.

They passed by a large patch of rhododendrons, overgrown and riotous, not yet flowering but well in bud. The bushes were still a sea of glossy, dark green leaves. The dog disappeared into them. A blackbird came flying out, giving its alarm call and a couple of pheasants scurried out the far side before taking to the air. If Dusty was investigating for rabbits, and he probably was, he was unlikely to be lucky.

Nothing grows under the dense shade of rhododendrons, not even a blade of grass and although they provide useful cover for all sorts of animals and birds, Greg knew from bird-nesting visits that these bushes had no burrows under them. The rabbits preferred a nearby bank in a roadside. It was a well-drained gravel bank with a long established warren. The noise that Dusty was making would have alerted them long since. Greg had already heard that distinctive warning thump they make on the ground with a hind leg when there is danger. He walked on. The dog would follow; whatever the distractions, he would always follow along in the end, almost as if he were afraid of missing out on something.

They crossed the road near to the rabbit warren, climbed over a sad old broken-down fence and onto a steep bank of beech trees. Tall grey stems took his eye high up to the canopy of new leaves still in their first pale green. Greg ploughed knee-deep through a drift of leaves from previous years which lay massed by winter winds behind what remained of the fence. In the clear morning air scents were keen and he met that sharp, musty tang of old leaves.

He was soon out of the drift and up to the top of the bank where he joined a hill road grown over with turf, which made it comfortable and easy to walk on. It skirted round the side of a rocky outcrop where Dusty wheeled and scented and rushed about like a thing possessed. Greg doubted if the rocks concealed a den, he'd never seen a fox there, but a fox had certainly passed by that morning and scented the place with its arid, pungent smell that goes right to the back of the throat. Whatever it did to Dusty it was not something he was prepared to pass quickly by. Greg left him to come to his own conclusions about the outcrop. In the end the dog decided as Greg had done that there was no den and the two of them carried on.

From the outcrop the road headed gently downhill. On their right was a long, slow slope of what had once been hill pasture but which now supported birch and a few oak. Woodland grasses grew in profusion and there were clumps of bracken and brambles. At the foot of this slope ran a dry-stone dyke and on the other side of that, a stretch of the main road they had earlier crossed.

Dusty raised a hare and followed it downhill towards the road. There was no way that a Labrador would ever find the speed to take a hare and the hare sensed this, bounding away on slow, springing strides before stopping half-way down the slope to check on the dog. To Greg's surprise the hare continued to sit almost as if it couldn't make its mind up which way to turn. A car appeared on

31

the road, driving fast with a noisy trailer clattering and bumping behind.

The noise put the hare off any notion of fleeing across the road and, with the dog closing quickly from above, it made a sideways dash to the right and opened up to full speed, ears flat back and skimming low through the grass. Dusty, too, put on speed and continued the chase. It occurred to Greg to call him back but the hare looked safe enough and vanished into a thick clump of bracken. The dog pounded on.

There was no cry. No yelp of pain. No sound. But just in from the edge of the bracken the dog stopped, seemed to jump back and then flopped down on his side, which put him out of sight in the undergrowth. The hare in the meantime appeared out the other side of the bracken and rushed on, not knowing how safe it had suddenly become.

Greg was amazed and for a moment did nothing. Clearly something had happened; no dog would ever simply have given up, especially after the encouragement of the hare's delay. Greg called the dog but there was no response.

He then had the strange suspicion that Dusty had been shot. That would explain the way he fell, but there had been no sound; he'd heard nothing. And he couldn't imagine who on earth would do such a thing or why. He'd heard of dogs being shot for chasing sheep or killing poultry. Perhaps there was a maniac farmer in the nearby woods who took pot shots for nothing, just for the sake of it. He looked frantically about and in vain searched the area for some sign. There was no one. Greg knew that he was alone. He also knew that something was badly wrong.

When he got down to the dog he found him lying on his side, flat down in the grass, looking small and broken.

Dusty made no sound but his mouth was pulled back in a strange grimace which revealed his teeth. He gasped and tried to swallow. His tongue hung out. Greg could see nothing wrong with him and there were no marks. None at all. He ran his hands over the dog looking for broken bones or signs of injury. Again he found nothing. Perhaps Dusty had run hard against something and just knocked the wind out of himself; certainly he seemed to be gasping for breath. Greg checked the dog once more and tried to coax him to his feet but there was no response. He then slipped his hands under him and tried to raise the dog onto his feet. It was then that he noticed blood on his hand.

Greg's heart thumped and his breath came short. Gently he lowered the dog down and examined the area between his front legs, low down on his chest. There it was, a small hole about an inch long, bleeding only a little, but deep. Greg could see into the wound. Again he thought the worst. 'Oh, Dusty. You've been shot,' he said out loud. He stood up and looked furiously about him, choking with anger and distress.

Sometimes you can't see things for looking at them. That's how it was with Greg at this awful moment. From looking about for some sharp shooter who didn't exist, Greg once more looked back to the dog and crouched again beside him. There it was, the thing he'd been looking for. All the time it had been just in front of where the dog lay and about two feet off the ground. Clear as day. The sharp point of a dead oak branch, hard as steel and weathered to a point like a lance. It was a million to one chance against, no, millions to one against, but Dusty must have bounded on to the stick at full speed and impaled himself upon it. Greg knew that he'd found the right version, knew that this was precisely what had happened and he looked at his dog and feared for him.

Greg, for a twelve year old, was of average size. Dusty was a large dog. Greg calculated that they were two miles from home; he could have run back for help but was very unwilling to leave the dog. Animals if mortally hurt, and Greg had no doubt that Dusty was badly injured, can crawl into the most obscure places to die. Greg had a dread of returning with his parents to find the dog gone. He decided, come what may, not to leave him.

He thought of carrying Dusty home and slipped his arms gently under the dog. But lifting him was extremely awkward and walking with him almost impossible. Greg's arms gave up in a very short space and the dog for the first time gave a whimper of pain, although he must have suffered all along. Coming uncomfortably close to dropping his burden, Greg put Dusty back on the ground and waited there with him, not quite sure of what to do next. Remembering the car and trailer he thought that he would stand by the roadside, stop the next thing that came along and ask for help.

It was a good idea but a painfully quiet road.

Greg stood there for fifteen minutes and nothing came along. He looked anxiously up and down the road, then glanced the short distance up the bank to where he had left Dusty. If he moved at all Greg was sure to notice. It occurred to Greg that any driver who thought that he was merely hitch-hiking would more than likely drive on. It would help if Dusty were also by the roadside; he may as well be sprawled there as lying where he was. So he ran back up to the dog and tried to coax him to his feet.

By some miracle the dog responded this time; he actually half-struggled and was half-lifted to his feet before taking a few short steps. At one stretch that was all he could manage; a few steps, then down again, then walking very slowly, dragging his rear quarters as if they had also suffered damage. Greg realised that if he took his time, if he paced the dog correctly, he might make it to the road.

Half-way down, a car suddenly came into view. Greg sprinted down to the dry-stone dyke and waved to the driver to stop, but he thought it was only some country kid being friendly and waved back, stopping not at all. Greg was now more than ever convinced that he and Dusty had to be on the road together or be stuck where they were. He went back to the dog who once more started his halting progress. Eventually, and not before they'd missed another car, they made it to the dyke where Greg gathered the dog up in his arms and carried him over before laying him down by the roadside.

'Get off the road, you idiot!'

Greg hadn't heard the Land-rover before it swept past. The voice was angry and as the vehicle rushed down the road, Greg thought he saw some brown and white dogs in the back.

By now poor Dusty had had enough. Close to where he lay there was a drainage channel cut into the earth verge and back under the wall they had just crossed. It was a stone-lined little cut, designed to take water, although this morning it was completely dry. The dog crawled the short distance to the drain and forced himself into it, jamming himself tight underneath the dyke. Greg saw what he was doing and tried to prevent him but the dog was too far gone in his misery to take 'no' for an answer and bit Greg on the hand. Not a bad bite, but a warning, a lot more than a nip.

This is it, thought Greg, wretched, lonely and close to tears. He's going to die. He just wants to be left in peace to die. He just wants me to leave him alone. But leave him he couldn't.

'Is yer dug hurted?'

Greg turned a misty gaze to the other side of the road.

'Was he struck by a car, maybe?'

The girl didn't wait for an answer, which was just as well because Greg wasn't able to give one. Instead she crossed nimbly over the dyke, which she'd been leaning on, and in a few lithe strides came over to Greg's side of the road. Without looking at him she crouched down beside the dog. She didn't touch Dusty but looked at him closely. Greg had never felt more wretched in his life; he was too grieved for his dog to take much comfort from anyone, not that the girl was just anybody. He had known at once who she was but his saturated senses could respond no more than they did.

'Was it a car?' she asked, again not looking at him but keeping her eyes on the dog; she gently stroked the sleek, black coat. Dusty made no move.

'No.' Greg's voice came from the back of his throat. It was painful to speak. 'He hurt himself in the wood. Ran onto a sharp stick.' Greg's explanation trailed off.

The girl had mousey blond hair tied up in a band; she wore a pink sweater, jeans and sneakers, all grubby. She turned on Greg a pair of brown eyes, deep brown eyes, almost black.

'I'll get my faither. Ye'll need a lift away fae here. He cannae bide here. I'll no be lang.'

She gave the dog a pat, crossed the road and ran like a deer up the same bank that Greg and Dusty had so recently come down with such painful slowness. She was quickly gone.

In what, even in the circumstances, seemed like a short space of time a van appeared round the corner, the engine coughing and spluttering as if it had only recently been started. It was an old white van with a blue wing on the nearside. At the wheel was a small wispy man of middle age, perhaps younger; a week's stubble made it difficult to say. He drove past and did a three-point turn at a lay-by just up the road from where Greg stood, watching anxiously as the van stalled. With difficulty and a cloud of blue exhaust, it started again.

As he drove up towards Greg the man at the wheel raised the fingers of his right hand in greeting. It was a simple gesture but to Greg it represented a solidarity and support which he badly needed. The van stopped so that the back doors were as near as possible to the drain in which Dusty lay silent.

The driver got out. He wore a maroon V-neck sweater with no shirt, an old jacket, which had once been part of a suit, and jeans. A hand-rolled cigarette jutted from the corner of his mouth; he left it there when he spoke.

'And yer dug's had a bit coup, son?'

Greg had never before heard the Scots word for a fall but he took comfort from the question, just as he had from the mute wave of a few moments ago.

'He hurt himself in the wood,' said Greg in a thin voice. 'I think he's finished.'

'Well, I wouldnae just gie up sae soon on a young dug,' said the man who, like his daughter before him, now crouched down to take a close look at Dusty.

'I'm no saying but what he's hurt, but he's a young dug if I ken onything and that's in his favour. Look, we maun tak ye hame. Whaur dae ye bide, sirra?'

'Just the other side of the hill. It's not far but there was no way I could get him home by myself.'

'Oh, but we'll soon hae ye hame the pair o' ye.'

The girl had by now flung open the van doors. Inside was an amazing collection of tools and bits and pieces.

There were lengths of chain and rope, a bundle of old bits of binder twine, a toolbox lying spilled on its side, various hammers and sets of pliers, boxes of nails and a small hessian bag full of staple nails for fencing, a coil of wire, a mel, that flat-headed sledge-hammer for driving in fence-posts, two pinch bars and a long-handled narrow spade for digging holes, a saw, at least one more spade and two axes. A battered thermos flask lay propped against a small drum of two-stroke oil and a pair of wellie boots in the curve of a spare wheel on which was a very worn tyre. Folded up beside the tyre was a tarpaulin sheet; the man reached in for the sheet and spread it on the road by Dusty's hindquarters.

'Come on, laddie, ye cannae bide here,' he said gently to the dog, taking him firmly by the rear and in one nimble movement scooping him onto the canvas. The man took the two corners nearest to him, the girl and Greg had one each. It was an easy matter to lift the dog off the road and into the treasure trove of the van. Doors banged shut, the van gasped into life and they headed for home.

As they drove up to the house, Greg's mother appeared. What on earth, she thought, as the van pulled in to her drive and up to the front door.

'It's yer dug, missus,' was all the stranger had said as he got out and opened the back doors. Greg and the girl appeared and Dusty was once more lifted on his makeshift stretcher. 'Intae the hoose,' said the man to his two helpers and without more ado they carried Dusty into the kitchen where he was carefully manipulated into the wide open basket which was his bed and his own special place.

'What's happened?' asked Mrs Blake.

'We'll need to call the vet. He's had an accident,' was all Greg could manage.

'Well, we'll no keep ye,' said the man as he folded the canvas sheet. 'He'll need the vet aw right but dinna brak yer heart, son. He's young, yer dug, and in his strength. He'll come aw right. Tak my word for it.'

The man and his daughter left the house and filed back to the van. Mrs Blake followed.

'You were very kind to bring them home. How can we thank you? Where do you live? Can we drop by and tell you how things go?'

'We're stopping at the heid o' the brae, there.' It was the girl who spoke.

'All right. Thank you again,' she shouted to the departing van but then thought how strange it was that she had never noticed a house at the top of the hill, perhaps Greg knew of it. She turned quickly inside. Greg was sobbing his heart out over his dog, who now lay face to the wall in his basket. She phoned the vet.

Vets are pragmatic creatures. They've seen it all and nothing seems to disturb them. McNab, the vet, was a large, heavy man who filled the kitchen with his presence. Even his hat and coat on the hall-stand seemed to take up much more space than a hat and coat ever should.

But he knew his job and seemingly with no fear of being bitten he examined Dusty from all angles, checking for hidden damage, before coming to the conclusion that the stab wound, for such it certainly was, was the only injury. He probed the wound to determine how deep it was before saying that the dog had had the devil's own luck not to puncture a lung, since clearly the piece of wood had missed his heart and had to go somewhere else.

The vet decided against closing the wound for fear of 'stitching in trouble', as he put it. He gave the dog an antibiotic by injection and left a supply of little tubes of the same preparation in ointment form which were to be squeezed into the wound twice daily. 'The next twenty-four hours,' he said, 'will be critical.'

Critical they were. The dog just lay there. He ran a temperature and scarcely moved. Greg's mother administered the ointment as per instructions and encouraged Dusty to drink a little water. He took nothing to eat.

The day of the accident, Greg's father had been away in Glasgow on some business for his new firm and did not return until evening. Greg and his mother were used to coping with emergencies in his absence but it was good to have him back. He was a tall, calm man, not given to panic.

He went into the kitchen and fussed over the dog, who managed to raise his eyes in recognition. He put his arm round Greg's shoulders. 'Dogs are not like us, you know. They can stand a lot more shock than we can. Animals have greater powers of recovery than humans; we're too used to being spoiled by the wonders of science. We've lost some faith in ourselves, but they haven't. I think he'll be all right.'

'He's on penicillin', said Greg.

'So much the better,' replied his father. 'But I think he'll pull through by himself.'

Alan Blake proved to be right. By the following afternoon Dusty, very stiff and obviously still in pain, struggled out of his basket. He allowed Greg's mother to support him as he crept out the back door. She left him. He sniffed the air, made an acrobatic attempt to cock his leg on the garden fence and crept back inside.

On Monday afternoon Greg came home from school to find Dusty sprawled in the hall instead of lying more dead than alive in his basket. His tail gave a few wallops on the floor in welcome. It was still a long way short of his usual greeting, but clearly he was on the mend. By the end of the week the supply of penicillin tubes had been exhausted, the wound was still open but showed signs of healing. The dog was slow but much stronger and his muscles were still too sore to allow a full-throated bark, but he was definitely on the road to recovery. In three weeks Dusty was a cured dog, with nothing to show for his trouble except for a small scar which became, in time, a patch of white hair where the piece of wood had struck him.

A few days after the accident Greg's mother suggested that he go and thank the people who had helped him.

'Good idea,' he said. 'I was definitely going to go in any case. Just as soon as there was something definite to tell them. Did they give an address?'

'The girl said that they lived at the top of the hill.'

'Where about?' asked Greg.

'No idea. I thought you might know. You're the one who's been over these parts with a fine tooth-comb!'

'Well I haven't seen a house up there. Must have missed it. I'll go up after tea and have a look.'

Greg's mother reached up into a kitchen cupboard and brought down a tin of chocolate biscuits. 'I got these yesterday,' she said. 'It's the very least we can do. I honestly think they saved old Dusty's life.'

Greg took the box in both hands. From the picture on the outside the contents looked lavish. His eyes lit up.

'Great idea, Mum. It's a fabulous box. I'd been thinking we should maybe give them something, but I'd no idea what they might like.'

The moment tea was over Greg left home and headed up the same road that he had so recently taken with

Dusty. Under one arm he held the tin of biscuits, now carefully wrapped by his mother and done up with a ribbon. In Greg's opinion the wrapping was overdone, but no doubt it reflected his mother's gratitude and that was something he shared.

But where was this house? It wasn't like Greg to miss so obvious a detail. The one house he'd noticed up this road was a farm and he was still some way from that. At the top of the hill he came to the bank of beech trees and opted for turning right along the tarmac road in the direction from which he and Dusty had been picked up. Still he noticed nothing. No sign of a house.

The road end to the farm appeared on his right, and on his left a hill road led into the top edge of the wood where Dusty had injured himself. The hill road was rarely used. Douglas fir had been allowed to grow close on both sides and were now crowding over it. The strong scent of their resin came to Greg's nose just as he caught sight of a thin wisp of blue wood-smoke drifting away on the other side of the trees. The day was damp and overcast and the smoke rose slowly.

Greg walked slowly along to his left, through a broken gate hanging off its hinges and down through the short avenue of fir. On the soft ground fresh car-tracks were clearly visible. Where his fingers clutched the tin he felt them beginning to wear through the damp wrapping. He moved his hand and held the box more gently.

It was the van he saw first, parked on the right just off the road. The Douglas fir petered out in favour of the birch and oak which Greg only too well remembered. There, nestled in the shelter of a rock outcrop overgrown with blaeberries, was the tinker's camp.

Between the van and rock outcrop sat a small round tent looking as if it had grown out of the ground. It was made from pieces of canvas like the one on which Dusty had been carried, flung over a framework of hazel sticks, bent round and tied with twine. A small fire burned in a circle of flat stones embedded in grey ash; by it sat the girl and her father watching two billy-cans start to boil. The cans were made from old syrup tins. Handles of thin wire had been attached to them.

The man and his daughter both noticed Greg's approach at the same time. For a split second a startled suspicion crossed the man's face, but was as quickly gone. It was Greg's turn to give a reassuring wave. The man stood up and gave a sweep of his arm in response. Both man and girl wore the same clothes as they had done three days previously.

'Hullo,' said Greg, walking up to the camp and feeling as if he were intruding. 'Do you mind if I join you?'

'It's yerself,' said the man. 'And how's yer dug?'

'He's all right,' said Greg. 'That's what I came to tell you and to say thanks. My mum and dad and me, we all think that you saved him. If you hadn't come along, he'd have been a goner, I reckon. Mum says she hopes you'll like these.' He handed the box to the man who, without examining it, gave it in turn to his daughter.

'That's guid o' her,' said the girl. 'Tell her she'd nae need tae bother.'

'Aye,' said her father. 'Tell here she shouldn'ae hae bothered hersel and that we're glad the dug's aw right. He's a bonny dug, thon, we baith said at the time. A bonny dug, we said. And strong. Powerful.'

The two sat down and Greg joined them. Had he known how seldom they received a visitor he might have understood their reserve, but the shyness quickly passed.

The billy-cans started to boil and splashes of water hissed into the embers. The girl produced tea from a small square tin by her side and sprinkled some into each can.

'Ye'll maybe bide for a drum?' said the man. Greg, of course, said yes and in a few minutes shared scalding black tea from the girl's tin. The biscuits were opened and passed round. Greg burned his lips on the tin and was told to take his time.

'Ye'll no be fae here by the tongue on ye,' said the man.

'Eastbourne,' replied Greg. 'I've been here about two months. My dad's in the merchant navy which is why we moved but I love it here, I love all the space and my mum and dad like it too. Mum thought she'd find a village dull but she doesn't.' Greg stopped, feeling that he'd possibly said too much. The man looked at him. The girl looked at the fire. Both listened.

'Eastbourne,' said the man after a pause.

'That's right,' said Greg. 'And my name's Greg, Greg Blake.'

'Well, pleased tae meet ye Greg fae Eastbourne,' said the man. 'I'm Tam Brodie and this is my lassie, Clunie, or ane o' my lassies. She's the only ane that'll join her faither on the road, the rest o' them, brithers as well, bide hame wi' their mither. But this ane's the youngest and her faither's lass.'

Clunie, thought Greg. Clunie Brodie. He turned to the girl.

'I've never heard that name before. What does it mean?' Normally he wouldn't in a thousand years have asked such a question, only he'd never met a girl like this. Just to hear her voice, just to be part of her attention was worth any question.

'It's a Gaelic name,' she replied. 'It means a green and pleasant place, a grassy hill side, it's the pasture on the side o' a strath or glen.'

44

Greg had often seen the name on local maps without knowing its significance. He was not likely to forget now.

'It was where she was born,' said her father. 'No too far fae here. There's a few Clunies if ye look aboot.'

'How long have you been here?' asked Greg.

'Twa weeks,' replied Tam Brodie.

'And,' Greg paused, 'do you ... Do you travel all the time? How about winter?'

'"Travelling" and "traveller" are no words I use, son.' said Tam. 'I'm a tink. I was born a tink. I'll die a tink and I'm proud o' being a tink. No just a tink but aw tink. I'm tink through and through and so's this lass.' He nodded to the girl and Clunie looked at Greg very directly in a way which said without words that she totally shared her father's pride in what they were. And the brown eyes went through Greg to the core so that he dropped his gaze back to the small neat fire hoping that his shyness wasn't noticed.

He would have been better to accept that the girl and her father noticed everything about him, including the nervousness with which he now picked up some of the sticks lying in a bundle beside the fire before putting one or two onto the embers. He laid them inexpertly across each other instead of roughly parallel. His sticks would burn clumsily and take longer to become part of the ash bed which is the heart and soul of a fire. He was also unaware that the guest or stranger never stokes the fire without permission, or without first being asked to do so. But the Brodies knew that Greg was unused to fires and wouldn't have known any better. He was forgiven.

Inside the tent there was a groundsheet of the same canvas that had been used for the roof and walls. Blankets lay colourful and bundled towards the back and pots, pans and a few plates sat near the entrance next to a cardboard box filled with groceries. A blue paraffin lantern stood on a small wooden box. Around the base of the tent several large stones anchored the canvas sheets and about a yard out from it all, a shallow ditch had been dug to take any rainwater that might otherwise threaten the snugness of the tent. Remembering the amount of stuff the van held, Greg was not surprised that the small tent appeared to hold little, although he had only glanced through the open flap and still kept most of his attention on the fire.

From a roadside spring, water gushed through a piece of earthenware pipe onto a flat stone on which a bucket could be placed for the few seconds it took to fill it. In the fireside silence, Greg could hear the water forever splashing. He felt awkward and wished that someone would speak.

'Do you stay long at any one place?' he asked.

'Depends on what there is tae dae. It depends on what work there is and on the time o' year. Ye see, we're kind o' half settled noo. The wife's better pleased in a hoose. Me though, I cannae stand being settled aw year. No me. When Spring comes I maun tak the croon o' the road and the lass here is the same. But no the rest. They bide hame wi their mither. There's six o' them, so they're aw right and so's she. Nothing comin' ower them. But us? We maun tak the road.'

That was only the start of Tam Brodie's answer. He and Clunie stayed in one place so long as the work held or so long as the local landowner would put up with their presence. The present site was ideal. Ownership of the patch of ground they occupied was a confused issue between the local County Council and a private estate, so they were able to ride out the occasional storm from either source.

Tam Brodie had a house in a small town about forty miles away, from which he ran a scrap-metal business. He liked the scrap business; enjoyed travelling round from door to door, farm to farm, shop to shop, garage to garage, although only small garages had much for him; the larger had more regular ways of disposing of their waste metal.

Farms were better. Farms often had their own workshop. Farmers' sons liked working with machinery and old cars and farmers' wives often loathed the untidiness which home mechanics and farm maintenance produced. So he did well from farms. Tam liked to bargain over the price of things, he enjoyed the theatricals of meeting people and of negotiating. He took a pride in being a quick and accurate judge of personality. In short, he had always had the makings of a first class tink.

In Spring he and Clunie left home and took to the road. If the scrap couldn't be looked after by the rest of the family, then it could look after itself.

They made hazel clothes pegs and willow baskets and sold them door to door. He took contracts to drain land or put up or repair fences. He had a reputation as a dry-stone dyker and, if need be, called himself a landscape gardener. He took on tree planting at so much per thousand seedlings and cut bracken in summer from around the small trees in young plantations. They picked raspberries which were grown by the acre on nearby farms.

In the tourist season Tam was known to appear at local beauty spots and play the bagpipes. Clunie would sing Scots songs or dance strathspeys, having first disappeared into the back of the van to change into a kilt and velvet jacket, grubby and unpressed, but equal to the occasion. Tam had an old tartan bonnet which he would bait with

47

a few 50p coins and wait for the rest to follow.

On the right day, at the right time, with the right coachloads of the right tourists, the bonnet did triumphantly, although it was good practice always to have it looking less than half-empty. 'Keep the bonnet poor,' was Brodie's motto and it paid.

'Do you ever get moved on for playing in the street?' asked Greg, intrigued at the thought of silver coins raining from heaven.

'I've seen us block the High Street doon by,' he said. 'What a day it was. Everything blocked solid and a tailback ower the brig, mysel on the pipes, the lassie singing and dancing and the bonnet near flat wi' the heap o' siller. There was scarce time tae take some money oot o' it or tae draw my breath. In the end the shops grew jealous and called the police but only because their ain customers could win neither in nor oot for the crush and confusion caused by us. I felt like thon Pied Piper.'

'Then ye should hae drooned the shopkeepers, faither,' put in Clunie, sparkling at the memory of such a day. 'Ye should hae led them oot tae the brig and telt them aw tae loup intae the water.'

'They were ower keen on profits tae dae anything bar lift the phone,' smiled Brodie.

'So what happened?' asked Greg, disappointed that the shopkeepers of Kirkbrae hadn't in fact been so charmed by Tink Brodie's pipes that he could have commanded them to throw themselves into the river.

'We melted,' said Clunie.

'Like snaw af a dyke,' said her father. 'We can fold up and move inside thirty seconds, but no before one last go round wi' the bonnet.'

'And in half an 'oor we were back and daein just as weel as before,' laughed Clunie. Her slim body shook with mirth.

'Monte Carlo,' said Tam. 'Thon was like breaking the bank.'

'Mair like breaking the bonnet,' said Clunie.

They both looked at Greg with bright shining eyes and he caught how close they were and how pleased to tell him their story.

With the atmosphere more relaxed he felt bold enough to look directly at Clunie. 'But don't you go to school?' he asked. 'It must be difficult if you move around so much.'

'She's no keen on the school,' her father butted in as if the question had been directed to him.

'I go when we're at hame. I go in the winter. But at other times only if I'm forced. The school inspector sometimes shows up and I hae tae go for a while but then I just go back tae goin roon wi' my faither. I dinnae like school and school disnae like me. I ken aw I need tae ken tae be a tink.'

She said what she had to say in a tone which let him know that she was not opening a debate.

'How old are you?'

'Fourteen,' she said. 'And how auld are you?'

'Thirteen,' lied Greg. He was four months from being thirteen but couldn't get himself to utter twelve.

Greg left the Brodies both happy and a little sad. Happy and pleased that he'd found them, delivered the biscuits and thanked them for saving his dog, and more than happy to have seen Clunie, to have been near her and to have glimpsed the life she and her father shared. But a sadness troubled him. It came from he knew not where. There were no books or newspapers in the tent, no TV, and he wondered if life were really all that comfortable. There was no sign of a toilet anywhere and both Clunie and her father had a scent all their own; not unpleasant,

49

but not very usual either; a mixture of wood-smoke and unwashed bodies. When he caught the odour in his own clothes as he made his way home, he was pleased; it was, after all, her scent; as much a part of Clunie Brodie as brown eyes, fair hair, jeans and a pink sweater which he now knew had a thin white stripe every four inches and a hole in the left elbow.

'Did you find the house?' asked his mother as soon as he walked in. 'Well, you must have unless you ate the whole tin yourself?' It was characteristic of her – to ask a question then answer it herself in the next breath.

'I did,' replied Greg. 'Only it isn't a house. It's a tent or a sort of a tent. They're a tinker family. They're called Brodie. I had a cup of tea with them and they told me about themselves or, at least, they told me a little.'

'Tinkers?' exclaimed Greg's mother. 'Why, yes, of course, that explains the van. It was just like a tinkers' van. Well, I never. Just fancy that. I should have thought of that.' She came close and sniffed. 'Greg, you smell,' she paused, 'of wood-smoke.'

'Yes,' he said, then added quickly, 'nice isn't it?'

'You did thank them?'

'Yes,' said Greg. 'I gave them the box. They seemed pleased. Said that you shouldn't have bothered. I think they went down all right.'

By the time Greg had given this information to his mother, Tam Brodie and his daughter had eaten all the biscuits, burned the wrapping and cellulose packing on their fire, kept the ribbon for tying something else and the empty tin as something which was bound to come in handy.

Chapter Four

A little more than a week after visiting Clunie and her father, Greg met Alistair on his way to school. He was standing on the middle of the bridge looking down into the water when Alistair caught him up. The small freckled boy also scrambled up on the parapet and looked over at the river, swollen and discoloured from two days' rain.

'Nothing to see today,' said Alistair. 'But I bet they're still there. Nobody ever seems to catch any o' thon six trout.'

'I only saw two on Friday,' said Greg.

'That doesn't mean anything,' replied Alistair. 'They're not always there. But they always come back. I've a feeling they never go far away.'

Greg was inclined to believe Alistair. Fishing was his one big interest and he did know something about it.

One day Alistair had brought a flat silver box to school, a slim box which fitted his inside jacket pocket. Inside were rows of little clips and on each clip a fishing fly, many of which Alistair had made himself. He knew them all, knew which time of year applied to each fly and where best to fish with what. He could even remember trout he'd caught on this one or that. It was said that he was able to scoop a fly from the air with his fishing hat, take a look, then go home and make an imitation from memory.

Greg as yet had no firm friends in Kirkbrae but Alistair was probably the boy he knew best. He'd been very loyal in showing Greg around during his first few days and they'd sort of stuck together from that time.

One Saturday Alistair had taken Greg fishing, lending him all the equipment he needed from his own extraordinary supply. He was patience itself but Greg was hopeless.

They started by fishing the stream which flowed into a loch about an hours' cycle ride from the village and after that tried the loch from the bank and eventually, come afternoon, they got a turn on the boat which Alistair had booked specially.

Alistair used a whippy, fast-action split-cane rod with a cast of four flies, but for Greg he'd selected a slower moving rod which he would find easier, particularly if he fished with no more than a two-fly cast to reduce the risk of tangles. Greg's co-ordination for fishing proved to be non-existent. The more he tried to copy Alistair's slow demonstrations the more frantic his efforts became. His line tangled, he jammed the reel rock solid, he caught the heather as he brought the line back and himself as he brought it forward. The fish were as safe as houses.

Not so from Alistair. He could throw a line anywhere he wished, even into the wind if necessary. He changed his cast twice, changed to a floating line, fished dry fly on the burn and wet on the loch, fished shallow, fished deep and had eleven trout by lunch-time. But Greg had no concentration and no patience with the finicky cold finger adjustments that fishing demands.

Nevertheless, he enjoyed himself; he enjoyed watching Alistair's skills, got excited when he hooked a fish and most of all enjoyed the place. A great deal of his trouble as a fisherman was a preference for looking about him rather than paying attention to the task at hand. In the afternoon Alistair changed Greg to a four-fly cast and rowed the boat while Greg drifted his flies behind; the lazy way to fish, but it earned two trout and a touch from several more. Rowing the loch boat was more strenuous than it appeared, as Greg found out when he took his turn on the oars. The freckled boy was stronger than he looked.

From their meeting on the bridge that morning Greg and Alistair stayed together all the way to school. The shy boy had warmed to various theories as to where the six big trout might go when the water was high and talked fishing non-stop. Greg didn't mind, he liked Alistair and even went the long way round to school rather than take his riverside short-cut which Alistair, for some reason, never used.

The school playground looked normal that morning, the bell sounded the same, there was the usual milling in the cloakrooms and in the crowded corridors. No more noise than usual, and no less. But in the actual classroom there was a big difference. When Greg entered the door, there, sitting in a front desk, was Clunie.

He gave a gasp of astonishment and was about to go up and speak to her when something told him not to. She had seen him clearly enough but made no sign of recognition. She looked straight ahead. On her face was a look of bitter resentment. As he made his way to his own desk he overheard whispers from the other kids which must also have reached Clunie: 'Tink Brodie', 'Good God just look who's back', 'She cannae even read yet and her near leaving age', 'Help me God', ... 'Sssh!'

With a sharp hiss and a rap on her desk with the back of a wooden duster Mrs Thompson quietened her sniggering brood. She was angry.

'You will see, class, that we have Clunie back with us this morning. I want her to be made welcome. I know that she hasn't always been fond of school but I would like that to change.' Then, turning to Clunie, 'You're a clever enough girl, Clunie Brodie, take it from me. This time we must try and do better by you.' They were kind enough and well-meaning words but Greg knew that they had fallen on deaf ears. There was an ugliness in the air, a cruel hostility which he hadn't sensed before.

Eager as usual to be first with important information, Alistair whispered from behind Greg that this was Clunie Brodie, the tink. She only came to school when the inspector forced her to and although she was two years older than the rest of the class she could scarcely read and write; special classes had been arranged for her at one time but she hardly ever turned up. Greg wished that Alistair would shut his mouth.

He knew that there was trouble coming and coming soon.

At first break Clunie stayed in the class talking to Mrs Thompson but at lunch-time she had to join the rest of the school.

'Tink, Tink, There's a stink o' Tink.' The chant, harshly repeated from the corner of the schoolyard, cut through Greg like a steel blade. He'd never seen bullying at this school; at least he'd never experienced it himself, perhaps because his fluke skills with football seemed to have lasted. He saw and heard it now.

Clunie was hemmed into a corner where the school gym jutted out from the main building. She looked straight ahead, hands clenched by her side as the jeering crowd, largely girls, kept up their abuse. Boys and girls usually keep separate in such matters although they are equally vile. But on the outer fringes of the crowd, a few boys lingered. Greg watched in agony. Something had to be done. Where was a member of staff? Why were they always so thick and useless when most needed? 'I bet they think that this is something which just sorts itself out,' Greg screamed to himself between clenched teeth. 'Well it doesn't.'

Clunie continued to look straight ahead. Then a large girl with long flowing golden hair, walked up close and spat on her sweater before giving her a push. Clunie's slight body lurched to the side but she turned back with her eyes blazing and seizing the girl's hair in her left hand she hit her a mighty wallop on the side of the head with the flat of her right. For a moment the crowd was hushed by the sound of the blow. Both they and the big girl were equally stunned.

Seconds later Clunie was fighting as if for her very life. The big girl flayed out with both hands and put a deep scratch down her face.

She then tried to crowd and barge in on the lithe little tinker but Clunie side-stepped and the girl tripped over and fell heavily to the ground. As she was getting up, Clunie kicked away the arm she was leaning on. The big girl fell flat on her face and burst into tears.

Big girls tend often to have big brothers and this girl was no exception. The brother in question had been brought to the scene with the information that, 'Tink Brodie's just gean yer sister an awfae belt in the lug.' The crowd parted as he pushed his way up to Clunie. Normally boys don't hit girls at school but things at Kirkbrae had just left normality. The boy struck her full on the mouth. She put her hand up to her lip and blood trickled between her fingers. The crowd, like the cowards they were, egged him on to strike again. For the time being he moved no closer to Clunie but neither did he move away.

Greg had no doubt that he was seeing and hearing a form of madness. It had to be stopped. Something had to be done. And fast. Now it was his turn to push through the crowd. For them, this was a new and unexpected development. Greg stood between Clunie and the large boy. The crowd grew silent as if by the wave of a magic wand.

Into Greg's mind came his father's voice, the voice of the tall, dark man. It told him to remember what he'd been taught, especially that simple is always best. It told him not to argue, not to say a word. If he talked, all that would happen was that his voice would go tense and high-pitched and his concentration leave him. He stood his ground in silence but his eyes told the bigger boy to back off.

'You goin' tae dae something about it, ye Eastbourne, naff, ye?'

The crowd sniggered. Greg measured the other and waited. The crowd grew eager and urged the boy on. Greg gathered his concentration and still waited. His father's voice told him that it wouldn't be long, that he was about to get his chance. The blond-headed sister had stopped her sniffling and screamed at her brother to do something. He walked up to Greg and made to push him in the chest before wading in with his fists. But to push Greg in the chest he had to put his arm out. The arm came out and Greg took his chance. He took it beautifully.

Waiting until the boy was moving forward, in one liquid curve he took the on-coming right arm and turned it into the simplest lock in the book. He gave the arm a sharp blow on the upturned elbow just to state clearly who was in charge and then, keeping pressure on the elbow all he had to do was to walk quickly backwards. The other boy had a choice between a broken arm and hitting the ground face first with all his weight. The choice, however, was in Greg's hands and since he'd already done a fair bit of arm bending, he elected to bring the boy down hard. Most people would now have let go of the arm and stood back. Not Greg. He'd been better taught. He kept hold of the captured arm and brought it hard round behind the boy so that the hand touched the back of his neck and he cried out in pain.

The crowd was quiet once again. They almost heard the arm creak – some said afterwards that they did. One thing they did hear was Greg's voice.

'I'll let you up on one condition. That you never touch that girl again. And that applies to all of you,' he shouted. 'Leave her alone!' He gave the arm a notch more for emphasis and let the boy up.

The crowd drifted away shame-faced, Greg stayed where he was looking after them, breathing hard. What they didn't know was that he'd never had to hit anyone in his life before.

Clunie too remained where she was. He turned to face her. 'You all right?' he asked. Keeping her hand to her mouth she nodded then ran to the school-gate and kept on running straight out. He knew where she was going.

Next morning, to his complete astonishment, she was back at her desk. No one had expected to see her again. No one. Her top lip was swollen and she kept herself to herself. There was no more trouble. That was the last of it.

Nature compensates. Nature always compensates. If someone is weak in one way, they are strong in another.

It was true that Clunie could hardly read and write, but that did not prevent her from being well off for native wit and intelligence. Like many people who have trouble with reading, her ability to remember the spoken word was remarkable and although she couldn't do maths because of all the missed classes, she was quick at mental arithmetic.

'It will come, this reading of yours,' Mrs Thompson would tell her. 'It will come when you relax and let it reach you. You've been shutting it out with the rest of school but perhaps that's changing. I hope so.'

Her hope was not entirely unfounded although Clunie was still light years from approaching school with open arms.

In one thing Clunie was brilliant. In one thing she was head and shoulders above the rest. No one could even start to equal her talent for drawing. One day the class had sat outside and drawn the trees along the edge of the school playing field. Everyone else drew flat, two dimensional, squiggly poor things, but Clunie's trees leapt off the page. When they went into the village to draw 'anything on wheels,' Clunie drew motor cars that made you want to dive out of the way for safety. When the class did charcoal portraits, the people who sat as models were horrified by the visions of themselves produced by this sullen girl who still sat by herself down in the front row. They were shocked to see how well she knew them, how frighteningly clearly she read their hearts.

It was the same with modelling. In her hands clay became alive, everything she made spoke and moved. Spoke the thoughts which all day she kept to herself, and moved with the energy and grace which was squandered and stifled at her desk.

She still didn't mix with the other children, but no one could have described her as lonely. She simply didn't want their company, didn't need it. It was as if she were putting up with them just as a thoroughbred racehorse might put up with a crowd of donkeys that happened to be in the same field. Clunie shared time and place with

58

the others but nothing more.

Greg was hardly surprised; he'd known from her first morning at school how she would be. It wasn't for him to seek to change her. But now and then by accident, if there is such a thing as an accident, they would share a glance and there would be in that look a bond of knowledge and memories held in common: an injured dog, a camp fire, a tin of biscuits, a wiry unshaven man, the sound of water running from a nearby spring.

'Now, do I have any sugar in the house?' Greg's mother talked half to him and half to herself as she pulled open the appropriate cupboard door and looked in. 'I don't think so. No. Nothing. Just as I thought. It's all bloomin' well for your father to say "shop just once a week" but he's no idea how easy it is to forget things. Sugar. Blimey, not a grain in the house. Greg, be a love and pop to the shop. It won't take your young legs two seconds.'

Greg agreed to the errand before his mother stopped speaking. It was a lovely evening, the light was lasting later and later and he wouldn't mind a quick stroll to the village. It was also a good chance to think about his homework instead of actually doing it. He went out the back gate and down some narrow stone steps which took him to the tarmac road between his house and the village. For some reason he felt like a change from the path he used in the mornings. Or perhaps he was meant to take the road.

'The lassie telt me how she came by thon sair mooth and the pairt ye played. Ye were guid, sirra. Ye were guid. Naebody else would hae cared aboot her; I ken that for a fact, for I've been doon tae that school tae complain many's a time. I've aye kent that she'd nae life there. Nae life at aw. But ye were guid and I'm obliged tae ye.' It was

59

several days since the fracas at school and more than several since Greg had last seen Tam Brodie. They met now on the road which was the most natural place for Tam to meet anyone. As he spoke he'd taken Greg's hand and shaken it for what seemed like a very long time. On his breath was the lazy, sweet smell of whisky and he rocked gently on his feet.

Greg wanted any conversation to stay on Clunie. 'Clunie's very quiet,' he said. 'Never says much.'

'She's like masel,' said her father. 'Likes tae dae things her ain way and no be ower close mixed in wi' other folk. If they'll just leave her be she'll dae fine. And maybe now they will.' With that Tink Brodie had said enough about his daughter. Clearly he felt that things were all right with her. You could expect a man to know his daughter but Tam always gave Greg the feeling that he had the right version of lots of things. Nothing book-learned but things seen from the corner of an eye, things heard casually, especially the small things over which people tend to be so careless. These would feed his judgments and give him an edge over staid and settled folk who thought him no better than a feckless outcast.

Tam moved to the edge of the narrow road and sat down on the grassy bank, snuggling into the long grass to make himself comfortable. He brought out a packet of cigarette papers and held one in his mouth while he found a tin of tobacco. Over the open tin he rolled a cigarette, nipping off the excess tobacco at either end and crumbling these small savings back into the tin.

'Tam, I've got to get sugar for my Mum,' said Greg.

Tam ignored the urgency. He lit up. Blue smoke hung on the air and trailed over the long stalks of grass.

'Tell ye an interesting thing, Greg fae Eastbourne. There's money in conservation.'

The sugar had to wait. Greg knew that the story might well last as long as the cigarette.

It was all about a local landowner who had a few acres of wet, badly-drained land which he'd put a deer-fence around and planted up with Sitka spruce. Sitka are quick-growing and it was intended that in about ten years the trees would be sufficiently established to be used as a shelter belt for sheep or beef cattle. 'Ye dinnae need tae keep beef stirks inside in the winter,' Tam continued. 'If they hae a bit shelter and enough feed, they'd far sooner be oot and aw the better for it.'

Hill stock should have a shelter belt in any case and this was an estate that caught a lot of snow if the January wind blew hard from the East. Before a snowstorm you will see sheep gathering close in behind the lee side of the stone dykes which divide hillsides and fields and on a bad night, snow can drift over and smother them, so they're much better off amongst trees. So Tam's story went on, concluding that this shelter belt, like all shelter belts, was essential.

But there were problems. The place was bad with bracken and even when it was grazed, the grazing was of limited value with the bracken pushing out more and more grass and carrying ticks which plagued the sheep and if bad enough made them ill. After the trees were planted the bracken came in with a vengeance and from late spring to late autumn hardly a blink of light reached the young trees which looked as if they could remain starved and stunted forever.

The popular and modern way of controlling bracken was to use chemical sprays. 'It's just one helluva job,' said Tam. 'And no ane that I would ever want tae dae.' Whoever sprayed had to wear a protective PVC suit, and gloves, a helmet, face mask and wellie boots and on his

61

back carry a heavy tank of spray which he hand-pumped onto the vegetation, which could sometimes be as high as himself. Inside the suit and rubber gloves the man sweated buckets and in spite of the mask he breathed the spray; the taste lingered on his lips and tainted whatever he ate. Of all forestry jobs, spraying was the one disliked most.

Not that those considerations would have troubled the man who owned the land. What troubled him was his daughter. Tall, blond, loud of voice, fond of horses, and in her second year of a university course in Environmental Science. When she heard of the plan to spray the shelter belt bracken she phoned her father pleading, insisting and threatening that on no account must he spray and that there must be some other way.

The usual way with bracken has always been to cut it by hand, but chemicals are cheaper than men and for this reason have replaced them. 'But this is only a small patch, just a few acres, surely someone could cut it for no more than the cost of spraying?' the girl had implored. 'Seemingly not,' was her father's reply, although to be truthful, he'd never thought of not spraying.

'And wha dae ye think got word o' the tale and straight away offered his services at a not unreasonable but lucky-just-the-same-tae-get price?' shouted Tam, stretching forward from his seat by the roadside to give emphasis to his question.

'You,' said Greg.

'Right first time.' Tam stood up and flung his arms wide in triumph. 'Me, sir, Tam Brodie, bracken cutter o' high degree. At yer service, sir.'

Greg was about to offer some words of congratulation when the sound of an engine screaming in low gear turned his attention uphill. It also caught the notice of Tink Brodie whose senses were better informed than

Greg's. Greg still stood in the middle of the road.

'Stand back. Get back, man,' roared Tam.

Tam pulled himself further up the bank and brought his feet sharply off the verge. Greg leaped to the other side of the road and stood with his back to the crumbling stone wall which ran alongside.

In a cloud of dust and without a hope of stopping, a Land-rover flung into view. Greg glimpsed a large, florid, high-coloured man at the wheel and on the passenger's side, a pale man with a long face. The driver needed all the room he could get and came over whisker-close to Greg. He'd seen Tam and touched the brakes, only a touch, the vehicle swerved then lurched past. Gone in a split second. The canvas back was open. In it were three spaniels, brown and white; they rocked together in the wild movement.

Greg had grit in one eye and diesel fumes and dust in his mouth. He spat in an effort to clear his throat. Tam, looking down the road after the Land-rover, sat grim-faced and angry on the bank. He glanced at Greg. 'You aw right, there?' Greg nodded and Tam continued, 'Thon's twa fools fae the Gates o' Hell which is whaur I'd happily see them. Ross and Hewitt, known tae aw and liked by nane, least o' aw by me. They're gamekeepers on Kirkbrae Estates and friend tae neither man nor beast. Ross is the headman and Hewitt's number two. If this wasnae a public road they'd as like stop and ask ye yer business. Ross likes tae be the big man and Hewitt is the most miserable-looking thing ye ever set eyes on. "Boss Ross" and "Hung Hewitt" is what folk call them. They're aye the gither and naebody else would want their company.'

He got up and dusted himself off. His mellowness was gone. 'Did you no mention sugar?'

'I did,' said Greg.

'Then you'd better away for it. Mind you, it's no every day ye need sugar. I've gone for months wi' nae mair than I could mooch and pick up at doors. If ye just ask for a twist o' sugar ye'd be surprised how much ye come by. But ye'd better tae the shops.'

'I agree,' smiled Greg.

He could easily imagine Tam charming sugar at people's doors when he'd called round for scrap or whatever and he could just as easily imagine that he wouldn't get an ounce if he tried for himself.

They parted, Greg now in a hurry. But after a few steps, Tam's voice stopped him. He stood in the middle of the road looking down towards Greg. 'Dae ye fancy a go at the bracken?'

'I do,' said Greg. 'I definitely do.'

'Right then. Saturday half-past seven in the morning. We'll be doon for ye. Bring something tae eat. We'll be awa aw day.'

'That's great. I'll be ready.' Greg shouted back.

Tam turned and made his way uphill, hands in pockets, leaning forward into the steepness of the road. Greg ran to the village.

Chapter Five

Greg's mother could have been keener on the idea of him spending all day with the Brodies. She didn't doubt that they were honest or that their kindness had saved the family dog and she had heard at least something of the episode concerning Clunie at school. It was just that she wasn't sure if she approved of the tinker way of life, which was her way of saying that she didn't understand it.

She liked things neat, tidy and ordered. She was troubled by the thought of a life where it was difficult or not important to wash every day, or to eat regular and balanced meals, or to sleep in a bed which was changed every week. Tam and Clunie slept in blankets that were seldom washed. They never used sheets and slept in their underclothes. How did they get dried out when caught in bad weather? How about coming home from work cold, wet, miserable and dirty? Tam Brodie must often have come home with even his boots soaked through. Wasn't it an unnecessarily hard life? And Clunie? It wasn't always possible for her to go with her father; there must have been times when she was left alone in that camp, which didn't seem right for a young girl. Mrs Blake had seen the place; to her it looked drab and hidden away. Like living under a stone, she'd thought.

But she kept her thoughts to herself. Best to wait and see how things developed. Greg needed more company than he seemed to have found so far in Kirkbrae and if he liked these people, then he liked them.

One thing she did do was to phone her husband on the ship-to-shore just to hear him say, 'Sure, OK by me. Tell him to take a first-aid kit though, he might cut himself and I'd bet that Brodie's never heard of elastoplast; probably uses cobwebs and docken leaves or something else from the Middle Ages.'

The van arrived promptly, still coughing from its recent start and with the windscreen covered in dew. Greg and his mother came to the door; Dusty rushed out and barked at Tam and Clunie sitting bright as buttons in the cab. 'Morning, missus,' said Tam and pointed straight past Greg's mother to some wisps of mist that still straggled across the face of the nearest hill. 'Ye see yon stels o' mist, missus. Weel, I'll tell ye. That's a sign o' heat. Tak my word for it. By the time they're gone, ye'll be feeling the sun. It's a day for loadin yer washin' line.'

'Is it a day for cutting bracken?' she asked.

'It'll be warm, lady,' replied Tam. 'But we'll no complain,' adding in the same breath, 'And is he bringing thon big dug? It's a guid place for a dug where we're goin'. He'll hae a guid day. Shame tae leave him.' And he shouted, 'How's ma dug?' down at Dusty who put his forepaws up on the van door as if asking to be taken along. When the van reversed away from Greg's house it took with it both Greg and Dusty; the boy sitting next to Clunie on the double seat up front and the dog rattling around with all the debris in the back.

They drove down river from Kirkbrae but for no more than half an hour before turning up a steep farm track to the site of Tam's latest contract. On both sides they had rough hill pasture; grass interspersed with whin and gorse, with boulders, with wet places full of rushes, with patches of heather and bracken. Scraps of wool hung here and there on patches of thorn.

Soon they drew in by the side of the road and stopped. There was a six-foot deer-fence on their left and a gate with a padlock for which Tam produced a key. Even without the fence, their young plantation was obvious. About the size of an average field, a green sea of bracken spread before them; a slight breeze moved among the taller fronds, but everything else was dew-damp and still. It was hard to imagine seedlings trying to grow with such competition. Easier to see why they couldn't.

Tam switched off the engine and Greg for the first time heard the rush of that fantastic silence which lives in high, open places. It was as if his head was being filled by a soft and delicate infusion. So silent was the silence that he could hear it. It soaked through him. Tam and Clunie sat still. No one moved. They all three listened to the utter quietness and let it touch them. Gradually Greg's hearing attuned and became more liberal. It let in the trickle of water along by the fence side, the skylarks patiently singing on and on above them, the calling of sheep and lambs from either side of the shelter belt and then the long, drifting, liquid trill of a curlew. Tam looked at them both but still said nothing, then all he said was, 'Bonny, eh?'. With the smiles which answered him they both let their breath out as if they'd been holding it for fear of breaking a spell. The dog took this as a cue to lick Clunie's ear and agitate to be let out.

The silence retreated further with the sound of their feet on the dirt road, of van doors opening and closing and with the scrape of steel on steel. Tam had found three heuks or sickles in the back of the van and laid them on the edge beside the open doors. One after the other he picked them up and felt the edge of the blade with his thumb before sharpening them with a special sharpening stone; a slim grey cylinder of Carborundum perhaps a little more than a foot long, about two inches thick in the middle and tapered towards each end. Apparently with no fear of cutting himself, he held the heuk in one hand and worked the stone with the other along the whole length of the curved blade, until it was razor sharp.

Tam gave a sharpened heuk each to Greg and Clunie. They took their sandwich bags and flasks, shut up the van and made for the padlocked gate which Tam unlocked. The bracken was dense and on Greg and Clunie, chest height. Dusty disappeared into it and could be heard snuffling and crashing about. 'Heavy on his feet,' said Tam. 'He'll no be easy lost.'

With the bracken so tall and seedlings only six inches high it was not easy to find the young trees. They were planted in rows, five feet between the plants and six feet between the rows; around the plantation edge were a few odd rows that didn't run neatly into the others.

Tam told the other two to wait while he got his bearings. He found the outside line, which he cleared for about ten yards before coming back to the gate and looking for the first row heading up the gentle slope away from the fence. He found it, started the first few yards then put Clunie on while he found the next for Greg.

Greg was horrified to discover how small the bluish green seedlings were and also how spiky to the touch. He could never have closed his hand on one. 'Planting these must be hard on the hands,' he said.

'And on the wrists,' said Tam. 'Ye cannae plant wi' gloves and every time ye pick up a plant it prickles yer wrist and ye must plant at least a thousand a day tae mak much o' it.'

Clunie was head down and cutting steadily, taking her

heuk close to the ground and piling the cut bracken in swathes behind her, but carefully, so as not to heap it on the newly-cleared seedlings.

Greg started his row, swinging wild and hard. The first thing he did was to cut an unseen tree in half. The sharp clean smell of resin mixed to his nose with the damp acid tang of newly-cut bracken. 'Cannae man,' shouted Tam. 'Tak her time. There's nae job that I can think o' that's improved wi' hashin' and bashin. Here, watch me.'

Tam cut with a slow, steady rhythm, eyes front, growing more careful when three short steps told him he must be near a tree. Not that they were always there.

'Aye, sometimes the trees are nae to be found. There's whiles they just die oot and often the fence is no just what it should be so hares, rabbits, sheep and deer get in and eat them doon. And often enough the rows just tak a swing and ye miss them.'

Greg watched how Tam worked and sought to copy him when in a few moments he was given his row back. Clunie was out of sight, forging a path of her own.

In the next hour Greg learned a great deal about physical work. He learned that it requires more thought and attention than ever he would have imagined. He learned how essential it is to work at a rhythm that suits you. Whatever breaks the rhythm is bad and whatever sustains it is good. The work is easier if you don't stop too soon or too often. Sometimes Tam would sing or hum to himself as he worked, but always a tune which suited the pace of his cutting. Clunie, as Greg might well have supposed, worked in silence. Tam soon overtook Greg, but with a word of encouragement, that by 'piece time' or break, he 'wouldnae ken a time when ye ever did ony- thing else bar heukin.'

Greg cut a few more trees in two before he found his

pace. He soon stopped wasting energy by holding the wooden handle of the heuk too tightly and learned to save effort by waiting until he had cut several strokes before stretching back to pile the bracken out of the way. In places it grew thinner and was left where it had fallen, but generally the bracken crowding the young Sitka was tall and thick.

Clunie was first to reach the top and after a short breather cut down Greg's row to meet him and help him out. 'Ye'll soon come at it,' she said, with a kindness which tingled down his spine. Then she walked on down the row until she found the top of a decapitated seedling; she held it up at arm's length and shouted to Tam. 'See they heids, faither. I doot but he's a thing on the coorse side.'

'Definitely coorse,' roared Tam now also at the top and they laughed at Greg's clumsy cutting.

Up near the top there was a couple of oak stumps, too old and moss grown for it to be possible to count the rings and discover their age, but perfect for sitting on. They sat there for a few minutes and admired their work. It was infinitely satisfying to look back down and see the three long rows. 'Aye, but we're in charge o' it,' said Tam. 'We're definitely getting in charge.' Dusty sprawled beside them.

It grew hot and Greg discovered what it's like to sweat. The perspiration ran stinging into his eyes and salt-tasting into the corners of his mouth. It ran down the length of his back and down between his hips. He felt it soaking at the waist of his trousers, at the back of his knees, and he felt his boots grow damp and tight. The atmosphere was humid amongst the tall bracken and the wet ground. Greg was working hard. The hot sun was up and blazing. There was no more mist or faint breeze. He cursed himself for not wearing shorts, and wiped a sleeve over his forehead. There was no choice but to carry on.

At the top of each line they stopped for a break. The bracken first cut was, by late morning, beginning to wilt in the heat. Greg had brought a flask of tea and a bottle of orange juice but had got through both long before they stopped for lunch.

If the heat increased his thirst it did the opposite for hunger. By midday, when they sat on the oak stumps, his sandwiches had grown warm in their plastic box; he ate half and gave the rest to Dusty. Then he found some chocolate, but since that only increases thirst, he left most of it. Tam and Clunie, however, had a well developed taste for chocolate and helped him out.

Tam produced a small primus stove and brewed up the usual two billy-cans. 'No fires in the plantation' had been part of his agreement. Greg went back and forth to the spring where Tam filled his cans and drank the sweet, ice-cold water. The more he drank, the more he sweated. He was yet to discover that he could drink less and feel more refreshed.

They brought coats out from the van but only to lie on and after the long drink and a mouthful to eat they stretched out in the grass by the oak stumps and dozed. Tam and Clunie were asleep in no time. Greg took longer.

He listened to the rasping, strident exchanges between grasshoppers; within a radius of a few yards there seemed to be dozens of them. He watched ants crawling through the moss on the nearest stump and couldn't sleep for the insects crawling over his bare back or the nape of his neck as he lay on his rolled shirt pillow. His hands stung where he'd brushed against nettles and he'd skinned his knuckles on the stumps of newly-cut bracken. A gleg or horsefly landed on his shoulder and bit him before he knew it was there, even in bright sunshine they were out, but nothing compared to the numbers which would have appeared in duller weather. The loud slap of his hand hitting his shoulder startled the dog which looked up for an instant. Tam and Clunie slept on.

Eventually Greg dozed off, but woke after ten minutes wishing that he'd found some shade and stayed awake. He had a pounding headache from the sun and the taste of chocolate in his mouth had turned foul. Dusty hadn't moved and sat up when Greg raised his head. Tam and Clunie woke fresh as a couple of daisies, stretched, yawned and looked about them, blinking in the bright light. 'I dreamed it was time tae ging hame,' said Clunie.

'Some chance,' said Tam. He stood up, looked about and flexed his shoulders from the set of sleep. It pleased him to see how much ground they'd covered. 'But we're doin fine,' he said. 'Twa and a bit days and we'll bash this bit oot, nae bother.'

The heuks got a touch of the sharpening stone at the end of every row and at lunch-time they were given an extra burnish. They might even get a rub from a file or have a point straightened out where a blow against a stone had bent it over. Tam leant across his bag and drew out a file.

He'd no sooner touched the blade when, 'Sssh, Faither!' came urgently from Clunie. He and Greg both looked her way. Even Dusty shared some interest. About fifty yards from where they sat, further up the hill on the other side of the fence, was a strange little bank of earth left by some quirk of nature when the land was first moulded. Clunie pointed towards it. At the foot of this bank were several rabbit burrows, with sprawling patches of light brown soil at their entrances and the pasture surrounding cropped close of everything except thistles and clumps of

72

rushes. During the quiet of the bracken cutters' siesta, three rabbits had appeared and sat by the burrows, just out from the patches of soil. The nearest suddenly moved off to one side and started to nibble at the close grass. The fence, thick bracken, and the benefit of the slope hid the cutters from the rabbits' view.

'That's my lass,' whispered Tam. He took a good but quick look round in all directions then slithered further down the hill before half rising to a stooped run and making his way quickly to the van. Again he checked for the unlikely event of anyone approaching before diving into the back of the van for a gun. To avoid noise he left the back doors ajar and retraced his steps. When almost back with Greg and Clunie he checked with a nod to the girl that the rabbits were still there and, still keeping low, moved to the right, nearer to the fence and cover of the uncut bracken. Greg moved down towards Dusty and caught him by the collar.

The report from the .22 rifle with its silencer had a long drawn, soothed quality quite different from the sharp crack of an unmuzzled gun. This new sound came twice in quick succession to Greg's ear as the two rabbits nearest the burrows were knocked clean over; their brownish grey turning to white as they lay belly-up. They kicked briefly and lay still.

Tam left the gun hidden where he had fired from and rejoined Greg. He took a good look round, especially at the skylines. Clunie had already scampered over the fence and had reached the rabbits. She picked them up quickly by the hind legs and ran back to the fence, pausing briefly to lob them both across before climbing over herself. This was all too much for Dusty who broke from Greg's grip and rushed to the fence. He retrieved one of the rabbits to Greg with about three times the effort a trained dog would have taken. The other was brought up by Clunie. Tam checked once more that there was no one around, then put both rifle and rabbits into the van.

For the second time in five minutes he rejoined Greg and Clunie. In his hand he held the brass-coloured cases from the two bullets. These he pushed with the point of a stick safely out of sight into the soft damp earth. 'Never leave they things lyin' aboot,' he said, looking at Greg. Obviously Clunie already knew such details. 'They upset gamekeepers and make them think somebody's been poaching.' With that, he and his daughter gave a quiet but triumphant laugh.

It was time or past time to start cutting again. The harsh scraping of stone on metal went up from where Clunie sharpened her heuk for the next row.

'Do you shoot much?' asked Greg.

'Never nae mair than the lass and myself can eat,' replied Tam. 'And I never sell a life. Never. I'm not known at back doors, hotels or butchers and I kill wi' the gun or not at all. I never trap and I never snare.' Tam had gone serious.

Clunie put the stone down and started to cut a new row. Greg had been banned from sharpening for fear that he might cut himself; Tam would see to his heuk. 'Fetch me ower the stane like a guid laddie,' he asked Greg, who scuttled over to where Clunie had been sitting. Tam continued to talk, from time to time looking up from what he was doing to fix a point by meeting Greg very straight in the eye.

'I just kill what I need. I detest the rearing o' birds and beasts just to have them shot for pleasure. I detest sold shooting and I detest its servants. I detest gamekeepers. It's as wrong a thing as ever can be tae kill just for pleasure

74

or tae cause pain by trapping or the wire. It spoils a man wi' life and it spoils the life in a man. It's bad luck and so it should be. It's the same if ye ill use a man, that tae will spoil yer luck. And I'm a man wha believes in luck.' Tam suddenly looked drawn and closed in by the importance of what he said.

There are two main occupational hazards in bracken cutting. The first is the ease with which you can cut yourself or someone else if you don't work in a staggered line; the other was demonstrated late that afternoon.

Things had gone quiet, no singing or banter, only the metallic brushing sound of the cutting, with now and then the clack of steel on rock. Suddenly Clunie let out a yell and Tam and Greg looked up to see her running from where she'd been working, swiping the air and trying to shake something out of her hair. Her heuk had been left where she dropped it. Unfortunately that was almost on top of the hole in the ground about the size of a golf ball from which poured a cloud of hornets, furious at being stirred up. It was a good ten minutes before Tam was able to retrieve the heuk and even then it cost him a sting or two.

Clunie had more like a dozen stings to her hands and face and was lucky not to have more. 'They're hot things, the hornets,' said Tam. 'And nesting in the ground the way they do, they aye see you first.'

Poor Clunie, she took it well, but her face and hands puffed up with the stings in spite of a sousing with ammonia which, by some chance, had been included in Greg's home-made first-aid kit.

'Aye, lass, but they're hot,' was Tam's consolation. 'It'll wear off,' said Greg but neither of them felt that they could say anything very helpful. In the end Tam made the best suggestion which was that they'd done enough and should call it a day. They would work round the hornet's nest tomorrow. It is not unusual to see clumps of bracken left on otherwise cut rows but anyone who had done the job knows without looking just why they were avoided.

As they left the shelter belt, Greg's whole body sang with sunshine. He was filled from top to toe with the deepest contentment and a fatigue he had never known. When he got home he was almost too tired to speak. Even the dog was tired.

Tam and Clunie had dropped Greg off at his gate. 'Ye did weel, sirra,' said Tam and pressed into the boy's hand a ten pound note folded small. Greg at first refused, saying that he'd probably been more of a burden than a help, but as he held out the note to give it back to Tam, Clunie had taken his hand and closed it around the money. After that he put the note in his pocket and got stiffly down from the van. His mother had insisted that he work for one day only, so Tam and Clunie would go back the next day and finish most of the job.

'You'd better keep this,' said Greg and handed them the first-aid kit.

'It cannae be my turn again the morn,' said Clunie.

'So maybe it's mine,' said Tam as he put out a hand for the box held up by Greg, who hoped in his heart, but didn't say, that no harm might befall them. Not ever.

His mother bustled Greg straight into a bath, he lay there, the hot water gnawing at his sunburned shoulders and back and the rock salt she had flung in the water stinging at every scratch and graze. By the time he woke next morning, Tam and Clunie had already cut the first two rows of the day.

Chapter Six

Mrs Blake had trained as a nurse and when she heard of Clunie's stinging decided to look up at the Brodie camp to see if everything was all right. The day after was no use because she knew that Tam and Clunie were back at the shelter belt, but that evening Greg and she walked up to visit them. Clunie still had a swollen face but was otherwise all right. Clearly she wasn't allergic to stings and none of them had gone near an eye or struck a nerve which is what Greg's mother had been anxious over.

Tam and Clunie cooked everything in one old black pot which that evening produced rabbit stew. The fire looked in especially good heart thanks to a few lumps of coal they'd found lying smashed on the road where they'd fallen from the local coal lorry. 'It's a bad day that doesn'ae bring something,' said Tam. Clunie and he moved over to make more space by the fire as Greg and his mother approached. Greg was apprehensive in case his mother would play the bossy ward sister but she didn't.

Tam and Clunie were pleased with themselves; the day had gone well and they had finished the bracken cutting. Tam felt flush and unless something turned up right away, he might take it easy and not work at all for a few days. Regular work was another thing which Tam considered capable of spoiling a man's luck. The trouble was that it didn't use enough of a man, parts of him grew over-worked while other parts became bored and stale. It wasn't for him; he'd opt for variety even if, at times, that put him hungry.

Greg's mother knew better than to ask Tam if he wanted a bath, but she did say to Clunie, after listening to an account of the previous two days, that she was welcome to come down and have a soak if she ever felt she wanted one. 'Just for her tired muscles sake.'

Greg groaned inwardly. Pity she missed Voluntary Service Overseas, he thought to himself and reflected that he might have known she would have to say something of the kind. He wanted to utter some quick cover-up or diversion but nothing came to mind.

'Oh, I'm aw right, thanks, missus,' said Clunie. 'I just hae a wash here in the bucket if I need ane. It's nae bother.'

Defeated on one point, Greg's mother tried another. 'Well, pop in for a cup of tea on your way home. We shan't say sometime. How about tomorrow?' There was a pause as Tam, and Greg and Clunie all thought that things were best left on their present casual basis and that a tea date was hardly the Brodie style.

'Well, thanks, missus. I will and thank ye,' said Clunie. Amazement struck everyone except Mrs Blake.

Greg was instructed to bring Clunie home with him the next afternoon from school, something which caused him some embarrassment. His mother didn't realize that Clunie kept herself totally to herself at school. She mixed with no one. She arrived and left on her own. No one took up with her and she preferred it that way. For Greg actually to meet her at the school gate and walk her home for tea was asking the impossible.

That Monday she was at school, but as usual made no

contact with him, something which in itself caused him no anxiety. He did, however, feel a twinge of worry when he left school with Alistair and was unable to see her anywhere in spite of the most intense, and what he'd hoped was secret, looking around.

'Who are you looking for?' asked Alistair.

'Nobody. What do you mean?' replied Greg, red as a beetroot.

She had vanished. How would he tell his mother? She would ask what arrangements he'd made to bring her home and he couldn't make any thing up; his mother could spot a flaky story at a mile.

All the way from the school over the bridge as far as the main street there were masses of children, everyone from the whole school except the one he most needed to see. He said goodbye to Alistair and headed up the steep street which led him to the path he took for home. It was empty. Sometimes he would meet an old woman out gathering firewood either carrying a bundle of small sticks or dragging a branch behind her but tonight the path was empty.

He decided to be frank with his mother, to tell her how Clunie was at school and that he'd never expected her to show up for a cup of tea. She'd only accepted to be polite. Suddenly, from behind a clump of elder, there she was beside him. He almost died of fright.

'Blimey. I thought you'd scarpered,' he gasped, but after the few seconds it took for him to recover he was filled not only with relief but with the certain conviction that he was now much closer to heaven than he'd been one minute before.

'I've been waiting' for ye,' was all she said.

'And I've been dead worried,' was all he could reply.

The cup of tea went well. Dusty, for the occasion,

79

doubled his efforts at welcome and Elsie Blake didn't so much as ask if Clunie wanted to wash her hands. Greg acted elegant and passed round the biscuits, he and his mother ate one each and Clunie the other nine. They sat at the kitchen table and felt fine. They talked. Greg's mother asked about Clunie's family and heard the story of scrap-metal, brothers and sisters and summers on the road.

Then by some magic difficult to describe, the tinker girl, with no trace of awkwardness, got Greg's mother to talk about her own family. In no time at all she was telling Clunie about her childhood on the South Coast. And the girl with brown eyes sat and listened and lived and remembered every word she heard.

When Clunie left she said thanks to Greg's mother as they stood outside the front door in the early evening sunshine. Washing flapped on the line. 'I'll mak ye a basket for yer pegs,' said Clunie pointing to the row of clothing. 'Next time I've guid willow. Next time I've willow guid and dry. Ye'll no get a green basket fae me, missus.'

In the kitchen, when Greg and his mother returned, Elsie Blake was quiet, and thoughtful and pleased. She ran her hand along the back of the chair which Clunie had just left.

'You know, that girl has something. There's definitely something about her, and beneath a bit of grime she's very beautiful. It's not just those eyes and my God, she has eyes as old as time, but in and around her there is beauty.' Greg had never heard his mother talk like this.

'Well, yes. I suppose she's all right. Don't know really. Difficult to say. But I'm glad you liked her.' He knew just what his mother meant but coming from her it felt strange.

* * *

80

From then on Greg saw more of Clunie. Not at school, nothing changed at school, but often on the way home she would appear on the pathway and they would walk together as far as his house. Sometimes she would take a cup of tea and sometimes she wouldn't.

The basket for his mother was made and delivered; a beautiful thing, deep and round. It sat in the porch full of pegs; red, blue and yellow plastic storm pegs and the traditional kind made from wood. In the evenings and sometimes at weekends, Greg would cut up to the camp and spend a little time there, chat with Tam, who was now doing a few weeks fencing or ask Clunie if she would like to come along for the rest of Dusty's walk. Often she did. It was a happy time.

The weekend before the last week of summer term, Greg packed sandwiches enough for both of them and he and Clunie climbed the hill behind his house, the hill which had been the first ever he'd climbed at Kirkbrae. Then they headed onto the long sweep of moorland that lay on the other side.

It was proper moorland; miles and miles of heather sparsely scattered with outcrops of rock or small, wind-blasted groups of Scots pine, gaunt and twisted. But not many of these; there was scarcely a tree in sight. In places, not even heather would grow. Carpets of moss, vivid green, purple and bronze when you looked at them closely, and a few hardy flowers like bog-asphodel with its red-tipped yellow flowers or bog-cotton bobbing white-tufted and indestructible in the wind, gave way to patches of water-logged black peat, acid and barren, where nothing grew.

'Blimey!' said Greg, startled as a dark-coloured bird about the size of a partridge rose suddenly from the heather at his feet.

81

Clunie laughed. 'Grouse lie close. Just aboot frighten ye tae death when they go off like that.'

'I'll say they do,' said Greg. 'I almost stood on that one.'

To their left a covey of about a dozen birds rose and made off in the same direction as the first.

'They're fast,' said Greg.

'No sae fast as they'll be after the twelfth o' August,' replied Clunie. 'Then ye'll see lines o'beaters waving flags, driving them towards the guns hidden in behind stane butts. The butts are kind o' shelters, big enough for twa men tae stand in. Makes it hard for the birds tae see them.'

Moorland grouse are encouraged by gamekeepers, who wage never-ending war on their predators. One of the natural enemies of grouse is the peregrine falcon. The falcon which Greg and Clunie now looked at was dead and hanging by the feet from a gin trap, which dangled on its short chain from the top of a fence-post, specially set up in the middle of nowhere. The birds need perches on which to feed and preen; it is not difficult to lure them onto a solitary post. Around the post, a few feathers, shaken from the bird's hopeless struggle, lay damp and silent in the heather.

Greg could not believe such cruelty. 'Who did this?' he whispered more to himself than to Clunie.

'Who dae you think?' she replied. 'The same as nearly ran ye ower the other night on the brae there. My faither telt me, Ross and Hewitt. This is on their ground.'

'But this can't be legal? I bet you anything that it's illegal to use these traps – and I bet this bird is protected!'

'No fae them it's no,' she. 'They just dae what suits them. They leave traps aw ower the place.'

'You mean that this is not the only place they use these things?'

'That's what I mean,' said Clunie. 'I've often found their traps. They leave them along the tops o' dykes for wild cats and at the mouths o' dens for the foxes. They even still use them for rabbits when they've a mind tae. No that a butcher could sell a rabbit that ye can see's been taen in a trap but hotels are no fussy and thon twa sell plenty tae hotels for drink or money.'

Greg felt sick. He wanted to bury the bird and with both hands he squeezed the shafts of the trap together so that the cold steel jaws opened and the peregrine fell into the heather. But he couldn't get himself to pick it up. Clunie would have done so easily but she knew it was already too decomposed to make it safe to handle. They left it, but not before tearing the trap from the pole and throwing it far out and forever into the surrounding heather. Dusty appeared from one of his wide circuits and sniffed at the dead bird. Sharply Greg called him back.

Greg looked about him and knew that the beauty of what he saw had been killed along with this bird. The pleasure and joy of this wild and open place was gone, its loveliness had become the clothing of torture and misery. The same suddenly applied to all of Kirkbrae; he couldn't look at any of it again without knowing that somewhere out there, it was possible that some wild creature was dying a slow and awful death or that set traps were lying in wait.

He felt as refugees must feel when they return to their native place to find their houses wrecked and pillaged by an invading army. The alteration is too great. It's better just to leave. But he couldn't leave. His parents were settled here and they liked the new place, the move had gone well. Up until now.

A black wretchedness drained the heart out of Greg as he stood on that moor and realised the full significance of what he'd discovered.

'Look,' said Clunie and she took his arm. 'I ken it's no right, aw this. But what can ye dae aboot it? Nothing. Ye can throw traps away when ye find them but that's aboot aw and they'll be plenty mair that ye didnae find.'

'There must be something we can do,' said Greg. 'There has to be something.'

Two miles away there was a loch, a beautiful place with lots of little bays; they had intended to have lunch there and spend time lolling by the water's edge doing nothing very much. That plan was now out of the question. Greg was too miserable to spend time sitting still. Instead they covered the moor looking for more traps.

Moving fast in high heather is hard work but Greg was grateful for something strenuous to do. Even so, they soon slackened pace. They found several lines of butts and a suspicious flurry of feathers but nothing else. In mid-afternoon, after some quick sandwiches and time to draw breath, which the dog needed more than them because tall heather is so hard on dogs, their luck changed. There, about three hundred yards away and almost impossible to see against the background of heather, was another pole and on it, they felt certain, a trap.

The closer they got the more certain they became, until they stood jubilant by the pole. Greg stretched up and took the open gin down to the end of its chain. The jaws, he felt sure, were strong enough to break a finger, he gazed at the ugly, brutal thing not sure what to do. There were no sticks handy with which to set it off by pressing on the little hinge-plate between the jaws. Clunie took the trap from him and knocked it hard against the pole. The jaws snapped shut. They tore the trap off the pole and flung it as far as possible. Greg ran after the trap, found it and flung it again.

On their way home they went round by an old dyke where Clunie suspected they might find some traps set for wild cats, but they drew a blank. They also took in a rabbit warren, but Clunie knew by the hard-packed, undisturbed earth that there was nothing set. However at that outcrop of rock above the beech bank, close both to Clunie's camp and Greg's house, things were different. It was the same outcrop where, weeks before, on the day he hurt himself, Dusty had scented a fox, but Greg had believed that the rocks held no den. Clunie could have told him differently. She asked Greg to call the dog in before scampering up to a narrow cleft high up near the top of the rock pile. She raised her arm in triumph and signalled for Greg to follow. He did, keeping close hold of the dog.

'Look here.' Clunie indicated an entrance not much wider than a rabbit burrow and well screened by blaeberries. She had a light oak branch in her hand, about the length of a walking stick and she ran this hard along the earth at the entrance to the hole. The trap went off with enough force to bite half-way through the stick and throw dirt up into Greg's face. He spat to clear the soil from his mouth.

'What did I tell ye?' beamed Clunie. 'And there will be mair than one way intae this den.'

They found another entrance with one trap close in and a second further out in the approaches. All three traps were spun hard round their heads and let fly into bracken and undergrowth.

It was a day which had not as yet finished with dealing out distress. Greg had accompanied Clunie the short distance back to the camp and as they approached the road by the splashing water-pipe they heard voices raised in anger. Just in at the start of the Douglas fir, where the campsite first came into view, Greg saw the back of a Land-rover and recognized it as the one he had so recently avoided. The three dogs were out and milling about. Greg called Dusty to heel and slipped a length of binder twine through his collar. Clunie turned pale and quickened her step.

Ross was tall as well as large and in heavy tweeds made quite a bulk. Hewitt reached almost the same height but the man was like his face, long and pale, lacking in lustre. Both men were much taller than Tam who faced up to them at the entrance to his tent.

'I've as much right tae be here as that stane,' he said, jabbing angrily with his finger at a nearby rock. 'And that's the County Council's stane and nae business o' yours. I'm bidding whaur I am until a better man than you can tell me different.'

'You're in my way and fine ye ken it,' roared Ross. 'This is Kirkbrae ground and the Council can be damned and you wi' them. This road goes onto our hill and if you think that I'm driving the laird and a load o' shooters past the camp o' some poaching tink, ye can think again.'

'You've no right on this land, Brodie and shift ye must,' put in Hewitt.

Ross spoke with a loud coarse voice, Hewitt's was high-pitched and timid. Like Ross he wore tweeds but topped the outfit with a deer-stalker hat in which sat a few fishing flies and a cockade of bright blue feathers from a jay's wing.

Clearly the argument had been going on for some time and both sides were rising in temper. Ross suddenly stepped forward and, seizing Tam by the lapels of his jacket, lifted him bodily off the ground and up close to his face. 'Get off this ground and stay off it.' Ross spoke slowly and with menace.

86

He let go of Tam and both keepers turned back to the Land-rover. Once inside, Ross stretched out his hand to close the door, but Tam flicked the arm out of the way and with all his fury slammed the door shut on Ross. The rolled-down window rattled in the door-frame. Tam stuck his face into the cab.

'A few hundred years ago I'd have shortened you by a heid.' His voice was white with anger.

Ross snorted in disdain and slammed the vehicle into reverse. Hewitt called the dogs back inside. The Land-rover sped backwards and once again came close to hitting Greg, who side-stepped out of the way. As he drew opposite to Greg, Ross stopped and looked at him very hard. 'If I were you, I'd watch what company I kept.' Clunie, they both ignored.

Tam was glad to see them and in peak form for voicing his pet loathings on keepers and all they represented. He was doubly glad when Greg and Clunie were able to provide him with more ammunition against them, although the traps were hardly news to him.

Greg's father was home and he told both his parents all about his day, sparing no details. They tried to see it all ways, that keepers had a living to make and a job to do, and that they had to control nature to some extent. But the reasonable approach was futile. They could too easily see the cruelty of the traps and they also knew that their use was illegal and that peregrines were a protected species.

'We should tell the police,' said Greg.

'The idea had crossed my mind,' said his father. 'Mum thinks were ought to contact the Royal Society for the Protection of Birds. I'm not so sure though; we've only just arrived in this village and perhaps it's better not to rock the boat. Why don't we sleep on it?'

Greg, however, couldn't sleep on it. The black misery which had seized him up on the moor by that awful post came back to haunt him. He could scarcely look out of their front window without wondering what agony the landscape concealed. He could neither hide nor deny his feelings and each day he grew more introverted, more silent and more unhappy.

In the end his father took him down to the local police station where they reported the incident.

'But what makes you so sure it was the Kirkbrae keepers, sir?' asked the desk sergeant. 'The moors there have been poached since anybody can remember. Maybe it was some villain, and they come from far enough afield, out for a trophy to sell to a taxidermist. A stuffed peregrine in a dramatic pose would be quite to the taste of some head office desks and ask a bit of money. As for the traps by the dens; well, that could be anybody, including farmers, there's a lot of sheep about here and shepherds are no friend to the fox. Oh, no, sir, indeed not. But I'll tell you what we'll do. I'll note your complaint and we'll keep an eye open. No doubt if we visited the den you mention,' he paused, 'the traps would still be in place and helpful towards our enquiry.' He looked knowingly at Greg who wished that he could drop through the floor just a little less than he wished he'd left the traps were they were.

As they made their way home from the police station, Greg's father knew that they had wasted their time. He could tell an official who would prefer to do almost nothing rather than give himself work to do. So all that happened was that the phone rang at Ross's house and the tired voice of the desk sergeant told Ross to 'get his traps lifted if he had any because he, the desk sergeant, had more to do than go traipsing miles to look for the damned things and if he found any he'd have to charge him which could mean paperwork and bother and they all liked a quiet life, didn't they?' Ross replied that he didn't know what he was talking abut, asked the source of the complaint, wasn't told, and hung up. He thought for a moment before deciding that he'd shift his pole traps along with the four others which Greg and Clunie had missed at the den, but leave all the rest.

In his naivety Greg had believed what the desk sergeant had said about peregrines being in demand by taxidermists and this convinced him to phone the RSPB off his own bat. What if it wasn't the keepers who'd left the pole trap? Another line of attack would do no harm.

Term had ended and the day after his telephone call Greg was at home when a fresh faced young man with a straggly beard called to see him.

'Hullo. The name's Hodge, Jeremy Hodge. I'm with the RSPB. Got your message. Thanks. Sounds as if something could be going on. Could you show me where you found this pole trap?'

Greg and the warden set out almost at once. Hodge was good at his job; he knew every bird and blade of grass by name and gave Greg plenty of information as they strode briskly along. He was also a shrewd judge of the public to whom he was much exposed and long before they reached the edge of the moor, he had decided that Greg was not the kind to invent his story either out of malice or a misguided sense of adventure.

Hodge was also a patient young man and when Greg missed his bearings on the open moor and became flustered at not being able to find the pole and the dead falcon, he remained calm. Naturally, the pole did its dirty work best if placed in a wide open space where there were no other perches, so it wouldn't have been placed near trees. Hodge therefore asked Greg to look around at the few clumps of pine and to try from them to work outwards to where the pole might have been.

The technique worked but still there was no pole. In the end Greg was lucky enough to stumble onto what remained of the bird's plumage on the heather. Most of the feathers had been removed along with the pole. A close look revealed the hole where the pole had stood and the heel marks which had closed it.

'I'm not surprised,' said Hodge. 'They've had a few days to get the news and remove the evidence. It's difficult to bring a case unless you catch them redhanded or in possession of traps and dead birds. We'll take a look for the second pole and I can tell you now that it won't be there.' He was right.

Jeremy Hodge had no doubt that the Kirkbrae keepers used pole traps, but he was just as certain that none of his evidence was good enough for court. What he could do and did, was to submit a report to his organisation stating his findings and suggesting that they put whatever surveillance possible onto the area, although he knew only too well how scant their resources were. He also visited the local police station for a chat, knowing that all he could hope for in that direction was to stir up a little more aggravation.

The visit from Hodge helped raise Greg's spirits. He felt that he'd done something, no matter how little. At least he'd broken the conspiracy of silence. But a few days later there was more bad news.

Clunie brought him a trap she'd found set for wild cats on a fallen tree over a small stream, near to where her father was fencing, and told him of her other discovery, which had been a rabbit held by the back leg at a warren near the same place. Just as well it was Clunie and not

Greg who had found it, because she knew how to put the poor thing out of its suffering with a sharp blow to the back of the head delivered with the edge of her hand. Greg felt helpless and the more helpless he felt, the more wretched he became.

But then he did a brave thing. Perhaps the bravest thing he'd ever done, and since he did it alone, all the more courage was required.

Early one evening, just after tea, he got out his bike and cycled the three miles from Kirkbrae to Ross's house. Hewitt lived with his sister in the village, but Ross lived by himself in a large yellow house down a steep bank from the main road and overlooking the river.

At the back of the house and clearly visible from the road were his dog kennels. As Greg approached, the dogs saw him and started to bark. His heart was already in his boots and the hostility of the dogs urged him to keep cycling, to admit to himself that he was sick with fear and too scared to see the thing through. He was terrified out of his wits, and who would hold it against him if he rode past the house and on to the next village pretending he was just out for a cycle ride? No one knew why he was there, so why not just keep going? But he didn't. He turned into the gate for Ross's house and left his bike there. He would approach on foot. It would give him time to collect himself. However, he was no more able to collect himself than fly in the air. His legs shook as he walked the short distance down to the house, his hands poured sweat and his throat grew tight and dry. If he opened his mouth no sound would come out. He wouldn't be able to speak. but speak he must. And soon. Very soon. He was on the doorstep and as if in a trance, had already rung the bell.

There was no sound from inside. Only the dogs, which

kept up their racket from round the back. He prayed that Ross would be out. That would solve everything. He rang a second time and again heard nothing. On the door was a knocker, a heavy, ugly thing. Should he use it? No. The bell was enough. He'd surely have done his bit by ringing the bell? He could go now.

He reached out for the knocker wanting to give some sharp, business-like raps, but it was so stiff that he succeeded only in giving one loud wallop. From inside Greg heard a chair grating on the floor and an inner door opening. Then the main door also opened and there stood Ross, still in his tweeds, but with his jacket and tie off. Even in his stocking-feet he stood tall. He glared in surprise at Greg, his face suddenly dark and suspicious.

Greg spoke first. It was speak or take to his heels.

'I've come to say that your use of traps is illegal and ghastly. You've no right to cause such suffering. You ought to hang your head in shame and if you don't stop, I'll do everything I can to have you stopped.'

Greg had run all his words together almost in a gabble. His eyes were full of nervousness and he'd half choked himself.

Ross said nothing. Then he pulled up the knees of his plus-fours and squatted down to Greg's level, although even there he was huge. Greg stared at Ross's third shirt button.

'*Illegal and ghastly*,' repeated Ross, imitating Greg's southern speech. 'Well, now, if it's not the wee man fae Eastbourne who's got nothing mair tae dae than go aboot wi' a scatter o' tinks and get in my road? Traps, is it? Frightened for a bit of blood and guts, is it? Tell me how tae dae my job, is it? See you, fella, there's an unwritten law which says that a man doesn't lift his hand tae somebody else's bairn, but if you don't get off my back,

I'll break that law with pleasure. Mind your own bloody business!'

Ross stood up and slammed the door in Greg's face. The dogs started up again and Greg, more in a daze than ever, went back to the gate, picked up his bike and made his way slowly along the road to Kirkbrae. He was drained.

When he got back to the village he couldn't go straight home, he was in too much of a turmoil; his mother in particular would notice and ask questions. Nor could he visit Tam and Clunie. What was the point of reporting another failure? And for all that they shared his dislike for gamekeepers, they probably thought he'd gone a bit soft on traps. Greg decided to free-wheel on into the village. He would go down to the river, sit on a shingle strand, and let the water soothe him.

Half-way down the High Street was an ironmongers' shop, closed at that hour along with all the other shops. For some reason as he drifted slowly past, Greg turned his head and looked into the window. He almost fell off his bike. There was Hewitt. Not in the shop, but in the window; a large coloured photograph of Hewitt. It was Hung Hewitt trying to smile, but even then he looked as if he'd just been cut down from the gallows.

Greg looked closer. *The winner of the McKay Cup.* Seemingly the shop gave a cup each year to the local clay pigeon club for the best shot. Hardly surprising considering the amount of cartridges, clays, guns and shooting gear McKays probably sold to club members each year. There was Hewitt, a crack shot to all accounts. He'd won the trophy three times in succession which meant that he could now keep it.

Greg sat by the river, close by the water's edge. Slowly it worked its magic. He felt his shoulders become less tense, he took a few deep breaths then a few more. He

93

thought of Ross and Hewitt and wondered why their cruelty should ever exist. He got no answer and his mind, exhausted rather than empty, came back to the river and danced with a haze of tiny flies across sheets of dazzling water.

It struck from nowhere. The idea came to him like a force. His thought were on the river, his eyes and ears were on the river and yet, seemingly from nowhere, came the idea, with such strength that it almost lifted him bodily off the shingle. Next thing, he found himself standing up with no recollection of having ever got to his feet.

Fragments of things said and seen came surging into his mind and they made up a picture so clear and complete that he knew it was the perfect plan, the thing to do, the blow to strike.

He went home, talked blandly to his parents about a cycle ride and the river and exhausted, went to bed.

Early next day he found Clunie and spoke to her urgently. She listened closely and after a few words she smiled. He spoke more. Then she smiled an even deeper smile with her eyes in it and clasped her hands together in certainty and delight.

Chapter Seven

Clunie began to spend more time at Greg's house. The two spent ages together up in Greg's room talking almost in whispers. They appeared to be making something. Just what, Elsie Blake had more sense than to ask.

Clunie had spent all of one day drawing. The floor of Greg's room was strewn with sketches. Every day small amounts of papier mâché were made in the kitchen and a large tin of plastic wood filler moved from the garage to the bedroom. If Greg or Clunie weren't upstairs, one of them, and sometimes both, were to be found crouched in the larch wood up above and overlooking Ross's house. In the course of one week they spent hours hidden in a clump of bracken which, along with a large rock, provided all the cover they needed. By the end of the week they knew Ross's working routine by heart: what time he left in the morning for Kirkbrae to pick up Hewitt and what time he returned.

The most regular thing in his life concerned his dogs. They were fed only once a day, always at four o'clock in the afternoon. It never varied and they were always fed on the same thing: boiled offal from the local butcher and a bowl heaped with maize-based dog meal which he took with a zinc scoop from a tall sack kept in a shed next to the kennels. Always at four o'clock and always the same thing.

McKay the ironmonger kept an account for Kirkbrae

Estates. It paid him to do so. Ross and Hewitt were among his best customers. They bought vast quantities for themselves; everything from nails to hill boots and each year recommended McKay's shop to their shooting tenants who descended like locusts and paid cash. McKay was therefore in the habit of standing the two keepers a drink when the occasion presented itself and Ross and Hewitt made sure that the occasion was fairly frequent.

Late on a Wednesday morning, towards the middle of July, the three were seen to cross the tourist-filled main street and head for the local bar. In the pub lobby there was an enormous hallstand, an old Victorian thing with the pegs made from deer horn. The stuffed head of a red deer stag with a full spread of antlers made up the centre-piece. It was one of Hewitt's few attempts at humour and amusement that he was always able to stand at the pub door and throw his hat onto the same antler. That Wednesday was no exception and Hewitt's silly little trick went smoothly. But when he came out a few pints later, the hat was gone.

Greg found himself with two important letters to write, one difficult and the other easy. Before she took up nursing, his mother had started to train as a secretary. Her typewriter was still in the house and so were one or two of her text-books, including a book on business correspondence. What letters say is important but often the impression they give is even more important.

Greg's letters would both be posted locally, he couldn't avoid that, but the important one had to give the impression that it might just as easily have been posted further afield. Business letters need to be written on headed paper. He had none. What he did have was some paper from a hotel in Switzerland where his parents had spent a short holiday while he was farmed out to his grandmother. He would use the materials at hand. He thought hard, researched hard, and typed hard with one finger. In the end he had what he wanted.

The other letter, the easy one, he typed differently, just a few lines and all in capitals. He read them both to Clunie who laughed fit to burst. Greg's mother heard downstairs and wondered what the joke was. Greg left the letters in a drawer for a couple of days. He felt them mature and grow ripe like exotic fruit, or perhaps all he felt was the ticking of time. After two days he was ready to take the long letter and post it.

The post arrives early in Kirkbrae. Next morning, at a breakfast table, the letter was opened and read.

Hotel du Parc
28 Ave Martel
Lausanne, Switzerland

Dear Mr Hewitt,

I have been staying locally with friends of mine and have learned of your astonishing win at Kirkbrae Clays. Congratulations.

I am a clothing manufacturer and have recently bought a company which is internationally known for the production of high quality outdoor sporting clothing. In spite of their present success I believe that this firm undersells itself, a situation I intend to change through a vigorous advertising and sales campaign worldwide.

Unless I am very much mistaken, you are the kind of talent with which I wish to arrange a sponsorship and promotional deal and to this end I hope that you will be able to attend a meeting at my lawyer's office at 23 Aberlenzie Street, Edinburgh on Thursday 26th July at 8.30 am. I apologize for this inconveniently early start. Please stay at the Waverley Hotel and bring me the bill

97

*and any other expenses, including first class rail travel. If this
date is not convenient please do not trouble to get in touch. I must
be in town in any case on the 26th and if you cannot make it, my
lawyer and I will consult our diaries and be back in contact with
you.*

*I would like to have met you before leaving Kirkbrae but
business calls me away.*

*Need I say that confidentiality is essential to our discussion?
Please tell no one of our arrangements.*

I look forward to meeting you.

    Yours sincerely,
    Ernest Sanning

'No like you tae get a letter, John, who's it fae?' Hewitt's
sister enquired both out of curiosity and concern. Her
brother had stopped eating in the middle of breakfast
and sat staring in front of him over the newly-read letter.

'Is it bad news, John?'

'Eh? No. No. It's nothing. Nothing at all.'

'Ye dinnae look like a man that's just read nothing.'

Hewitt grew angry. 'Well nothing's what it is, just a lot
o' havers fae a fella I kent in the army. He was aye the
same. Plenty o' nothing tae say. Anyway I can hardly read
his writing.

'Looks like it was typed tae me, John.'

'The signature, woman!' yelled Hewitt. 'I can hardly
read his name!' Hewitt was really flustered but with
emotions entirely new to him. He closed his eyes. The
letter shook in his hands.

He saw himself, John Hewitt, striding up the steps into
Concorde *en route* to another international competition.
On his arm was a pretty girl and in his pocket plastic cards
for bank accounts as deep as the sea. He saw his
photograph in magazines, newspapers and on television.

He saw close-up footage of a special series, 'Hewitt Shoots'. He heard his voice on the radio advertising outdoor clothing and giving accounts of matches hanging on the last shot. He saw the headline, 'Crack shot takes aim on sales bonanza' or something like that, he knew how the press polished things up.

Hewitt opened his eyes, asked his sister what she was gawking at, put the letter into his jacket pocket and knew himself to be a man changed, not just a little, but changed completely. When Ross picked him up half an hour later, he collected a man who no longer gave a damn.

As the twelfth of August draws close, keepers become tense, understandably, for it's the biggest day of their year. But Hewitt seemed unconcerned and indifferent. He appeared not to be listening to a word from Ross, forgot the simplest things, and did the most absurd, such as washing and shining up the Land-rover instead of walking out onto the hill to check the drainage on some butts as he'd been told. Worse and strangest of all, he started to answer back to Ross. Ross didn't like it and told him so, straight. Hewitt didn't care and said so, also straight.

One week after the letter had arrived, Hewitt, without permission from Ross, came home early from work. He washed, changed into his best tweed suit, produced good hill shoes polished to blazing point and a new game-bag which was clearly going to serve as a suit-case because he placed into it all the things a man needs for an overnight stay.

His sister was now convinced that her brother's strange behaviour was down to some woman and since it had all started with a typed letter it was obvious that he'd fallen into the clutches of a secretary. His words of farewell only increased her suspicions.

'I'm away on my ane business for once. If anybody asks, tell them you've no idea where I am and if Ross asks, tell him to find a new man. No – wait. Tell him to go to hell. I'll tell him myself about the new man.'

Hewitt drove twenty miles to the nearest station, took the train to Edinburgh, and walked out of the station and up to Princes Street feeling the very figure of a man. He made his way into the Waverley Hotel but not before being photographed by some Japanese tourists. It is not at all usual to see a man in plus-fours, new deerstalker, hill shoes and a game-bag in the middle of Edinburgh, but to Hewitt it was an omen of photo sessions to come.

In the hotel he made an idiot of himself. He called the receptionist 'girlie', ordered a 'big meaty pint' when the wine waiter showed him the list and shouted 'make it twa pints' before the poor man had left the dining-room. He ate like a pig and scoffed three different sweets from the trolley and all on the same plate. He was rude to two fellow diners over their lack of dress sense and ended by having far too much to drink. All through his meal a letter lay before him on the table, which from time to time he read, his eyes lingering on the word 'talent' and on the Swiss address, hallmark of those who travelled and understood large earnings.

Ross was in a filthy mood, not only had Hewitt gone half mad on him at the worst possible time of year, but now he'd disappeared. He'd called at the house as usual but found only Hewitt's sister who claimed that Hewitt had been away all night and that she'd no idea where he was. The head-keeper on Kirkbrae Estates was disinclined to believe her, but had no option. What the under-keepers' sister had said was actually true, but she was too afraid of her brother to add any details of her own.

Ross sulked heavily back to the Land-rover and roared up the road to his place. Perhaps that fool Hewitt had turned up there. If so he'd get a piece of his mind.

There was, of course, no Hewitt at Ross's house, but what had turned up was a slim envelope with a local postmark dated the previous day, the day Hewitt had disappeared. He tore it open. The letter bore only three lines. All simple.

Keepers are great men 'tis said
But can they always keep the head?
Trapping spoils your luck.

Ross scowled at the lines held in his large hands and reread them. Several times he reread them. He didn't like the letter, if that's what it was, didn't like the feeling it gave him. The feeling that someone was watching him, reading the letter over his shoulder. He took a quick look around the empty room. Suddenly he crumpled the letter up and flung it onto the embers still warm in the grate. It was a gesture of defiance and contempt. The paper charred, smouldered, then burst into flames.

'That's the best place for the lot o' ye,' Ross said into the fireplace.

At the same time as Ross had arrived home to his letter, Hewitt had paid off a taxi at the end of Aberlenzie Street and prepared to walk the history-making distance to number twenty-three. It didn't look much like the kind of street that a lawyer might choose for his offices, but never mind, this was a very hush-hush business, as the letter had said.

What the letter hadn't made clear was that 23 Aberlenzie Street was an empty warehouse with a notice outside saying that it was about to be converted into flats.

Some months previously, Greg's father had been asked

by his company to check if the warehouse were suitable for storing some of their equipment.

Hewitt gaped at the sign and then back to the letter and realised that something was wrong. Something was very wrong.

Ross had a full day's work to do and knew that he would have to do it himself. He also had a nagging suspicion as to who had sent him the letter. Who was it, he mused, who'd wished to shorten him by a head and who'd been kicking up a fuss about a few traps? Sometime along the day he would decide what action to take. Bristling, he left the house.

But the action which that day was to have most influence on Ross was already primed and set in motion.

No one had been reading over his shoulder, but from the hide in the wood above, Greg and Clunie kept watch on the house until they saw their man leave. With Clunie staying as lookout, Greg now ran down to the roadside, paused for a moment behind a pile of larch logs, then nipped across the road and into some rhododendrons which grew between the road and Ross's kennels. They were tall grown and provided little cover but they were all he had.

He came out the other side of the bushes, down past a row of four beehives, past the kennels and up to the door of the shed in which Ross stored his dog-meal. The shed wasn't locked. Only a piece of kindling wood stuck into the door clasp held it shut. When Greg let himself into the shed he was carrying something in a polythene bag under his arm. When he came out, the bag was folded into his pocket. He paused at the roadside before leaving the bushes. Clunie gave the all-clear and quickly he rejoined her.

From then until late afternoon there was nothing to do but wait. They were hopeless at waiting. It was the longest day of their lives, but in plenty of time for four o'clock they were back in position in the larch wood. The atmosphere had changed since morning, they were string-tight, tense as cats, every nerve and fibre straining.

'He mustn't pick it up,' whispered Clunie, although there was no one to hear other than Greg.

'He won't. It's too good. One look will do him. He'll leave it where it is.' Greg spoke through tight lips.

'He's going to have to.'

'Ssh. Here he comes.' Greg put a hand out and seized Clunie's arm as if Ross could hear her as he stormed past in the Land-rover coming from Kirkbrae. He turned into the house. They then witnessed what they had seen many times before, only today it was different.

About fifteen minutes after Ross had drawn up at the front of the house he appeared at the back, surrounded by the dogs which he always fed in their kennels. They milled around and got in his feet. He cursed and came close to spilling the pot of low-grade meat he held in one hand. As usual, he opened the shed door and went in. There was a wide ledge inside on which he placed the pot to keep it out of the dog's reach.

Greg and Clunie waited in an agony of expectation. They both shook and trembled. Suddenly the shed door burst open and out staggered Ross, ashen-faced and staring. He lurched towards the house and half-fell inside.

'Action,' hissed Greg and in a rerun of that morning, headed for the shed. This time a couple of cars came by and he lost valuable seconds sprawled behind the larch posts.

He knew what Ross was doing and how long it would take him but he couldn't guarantee that he would not

103

come back out.

This time he pounded over the road and down past the kennels. The dogs were out and barking, but no matter. Nothing mattered except for reaching the shed and finishing the job. Naturally, the shed was open and he went straight to the tall, half-empty sack. He put his hand into the sack and from it withdrew Hewitt's head, complete with deerstalker and blue jay feathers.

The likeness was uncanny, it was Hewitt to perfection, but only truly horrifying to someone who didn't know or who had forgotten about Clunie's artistic talents. Given the polystyrene base used for storing Elsie Blake's fun wig, plus parts of the wig suitably dyed, some make-up and a lick of paint on the papier mâché and plastic wood, she had produced a Hewitt frighteningly like the real thing.

Greg unfolded the polythene shopping bag, stuffed the head into it, checked the meal sack to see that no clue remained, waited at the door for a split second to check for Ross, then ran for it.

Calamity struck just a few steps out from the shed where one of the dogs got mixed up in his feet and sent him heavily against a beehive. The hive toppled over into three parts and more bees than he'd ever thought possible boiled out. He kept going up to the rhododendrons but there stopped. He couldn't leave the hive. Not as it was. Ross would suspect something for sure. He would have to do something about it and that could only mean putting it back together.

Beekeepers, for good reason, wear special clothing. But Greg had no choice. He put the bag down amongst the bushes and ran back into the maelstrom below. It was difficult to get a grip of the sections and it took him long seconds to put the hive back. There was no point in counting stings, so he tried to shut his mind to the torment and keep going. If he'd stopped to consider his position he would have gone mad. There were bees in his hair, inside his shirt, up his legs and inside his shoes. Even when he was safely back with Clunie his clothing still buzzed and he had to rub his hands all over himself in slow determined strokes to crush the last of them. Clunie did what she could to help and she too got stung.

They had to press on. Greg was too sore to care but he knew that the plan had worked. As fast as they could go, they threaded their way up hill to where two bikes were hidden in undergrowth beside a forest road. They pushed onto the road and pedalled like fury. Shortly, the sound of a police siren filtered up from the main road.

Tam was expecting them and had an extra large fire going. As soon as they arrived he took the bag from Greg and placed Hewitt's head in the middle of the flames. In no time at all the masterpiece was gone. Soon nothing remained but the stones which had given it weight.

Greg could scarcely see from his swollen eyes, but nothing could restrain the joy of even a blurred vision of the last of Hewitt. Clunie had found some ammonia in what was left of the first-aid kit and applied it to Greg's stings. Tam listened quietly to their story. Then he took Greg gently by the wrist and said, 'We'd better tell yer mither it was hornets.'

'Good idea,' said Greg.

Chapter Eight

When the phone rang in Kirkbrae Police Station it was the desk sergeant who answered.

'Get up here at once. There's been a murder,' said the voice.

'That you, Ross?' said the sergeant. He thought he recognized the voice but not the unfamiliar fever of agitation. The tone of shock.

'It's Hewitt. Somebody's cut the head off him. His sister said this morning that she'd no idea where he'd gone and I've just come on his head in the kennels. Get yourself up here man!' Ross hung up.

Standing next to the sergeant was an officer of higher rang; his Chief Superintendent had just dropped in on a routine but unannounced inspection. It's an ill wind thought the sergeant, who would now have more to show the Chief Super than the Sheep Dip Inspection Log. The sergeant spoke to the Chief Superintendent in a voice which suggested that he held down the biggest police job in Scotland.

'Murder report, sir, just in. Kirkbrae Estates, West Lodge. That was the keeper. Says he's found a body or maybe just part of a body. Something about a head.'

The sergeant, Chief Super and a constable drove to Ross's house at breakneck speed. The car jammed to a halt outside the house, the doors flung open and the three men made for the front door, which was opened by

Ross looking absolutely awful.

'And what's this I hear?' said the sergeant.

'It's Hewitt,' gasped Ross. 'As sure as I'm standing here, his head is in wi' the dog-meal. I saw it with my very eyes.'

'Kennels round the back?' asked the sergeant although he knew the answer. Ross nodded.

'Constable – stay here with Mr Ross. If he's up to making a statement take it down.' Then, with a 'This way, sir,' to the Chief Super, the two made their way round to the back of the house.

The dogs, by now growing hungry, acted up and made more din than ever. One of the beehives, if the two had the attention to notice, looked by the clustering round the entrance as if it were about to swarm, which was strange at this time of day, since it was much too late for a swarm to come off. The policemen, however, could be forgiven their single-mindedness. Ross had cut a dramatic and convincing figure and they approached the shed prepared to find the worst.

What they found was a pot of cold dog-meat and a half-empty bag of meal. No bloodstains. No sign of violence. They looked behind everything movable, checked around and under the shed, then in and around the kennels and finally the surrounding bushes. No head was found.

'You said that you'd found a severed head in a bag of dog-meal?' The Chief Superintendent spoke to Ross, slowly and deliberately.

'Not just a head. Hewitt's head.' Ross sat at his kitchen table, tightly gripping the edge. 'The scoop came up against it when I went in for meal. It's him aw right. I'd ken him anywhere by the hat. It was definitely Hewitt. Definitely!'

Ross now lost control and started to shout. 'And I ken who's killed him! They Brodie tinks and that daft English laddie who's taken up wi' them! They've been at me to stop using traps.'

'You admit the use of gin traps?' put in the Sergeant.

'Yes!' screamed Ross, in no mood to be interrupted. 'And I'd a threatening letter this morning. They've killed him. Killed a man over a few bit hawks. Good God Almighty.'

'A threatening letter,' said the Chief Super. 'May we see it?'

'Certainly,' Ross blustered. 'Certainly. Only, you see. Well. I burned it. Threw it in the fire. Anybody would have done the same.'

'I doubt that, sir,' said the Chief Super coldly. 'Not a letter of quite that nature.'

The three police officers said nothing for a moment while Ross tried without much success to collect himself. Then, judging his moment, the sergeant said, 'If you think you're able for it. Would you show us where you found this head?'

Ross rolled his eyes wildly round the room then swept to his feet and out the back door followed by the others. When faced with the meal-bag he was unable to look inside, so he seized it by the corners and tipped the contents over the shed floor. A drift of maize flakes slumped out but there was no sign of a head. Ross gaped dumbfounded. The policemen looked from one to the other and the dogs moved in and started to lick and nuzzle at the meal.

Back in the house, Ross made what statement he could while the Chief Super phoned for enough men to make a thorough search of the area. Ross had broken down and sobbed that this was no time to call a man a liar which, in fact, no one had said he was, although the air was heavy with the unspoken belief that the truth wasn't in him.

The police search requested was assembled but never actually deployed. Hewitt's head was spotted along with the rest of Hewitt by the driver of a police mini-bus taking the search-party through Kirkbrae *en route* for the scene of the crime. The driver had almost collided with a small car driven by the murdered man himself, who was trying desperately to slink back home unobserved.

No one ever learned of the real reason for Hewitt's mysterious absence, it was a secret he kept forever locked in his narrow heart along with the exact amount of money the expedition had cost him. The length of time it took him to recover from the experience matched his sister's estimate as to how long it would take him to get over being jilted by some dreadful woman.

The real pain for Ross and Hewitt was the publicity the strange affair received in the village. There was no one who didn't know the story of Ross finding Hewitt's head and no one who didn't know that somehow or other, Hewitt had also made an incredible fool of himself.

Hewitt stayed inside for several days before sending word to Ross that he had resigned and would not be coming back. In time he took a job as a gardener at half his previous wage, but with the advantage that around the garden was a high wall which secluded it from the rest of Kirkbrae. Hewitt felt safer behind his wall.

Ross likewise lay low as much as he could, trying hard to deny to himself his new reputation as an hallucinating idiot. For him it wasn't easy. The grouse season was about to start and he was still the head keeper, so he couldn't hide indoors or find a walled garden. He must face the world. But he faced it badly and in the wrong way. His swagger was gone and replaced by the most fragile of foul tempers. He could look no one in the eyes and coped only with curses and threats which all who heard knew to be empty. All, that is, except the American lady, a house guest of the owner of Kirkbrae Estates, who burst into tears when Ross screamed at her in front of the entire shooting party that, 'she should shoot straight or get off the hill and back to some cocktail bar where she belonged.'

The owner, a man in his late sixties, a small, deadly man with grey-black hair swept straight back and horn-rimmed glasses, crossed to Ross and stood in front of him.

'I'm the head keeper,' shouted Ross, sensing that his end was near but still taken by surprise.

The man said nothing but looked at Ross with eyes which went straight through him. Ross had never liked those eyes.

'I'm in charge until the shooting party's back at the lodge,' cried Ross.

'Watch my lips closely,' said the man.

Ross just stared at him. No one moved or said a word.

'You, Ross, are one fired gamekeeper. Get off this hill and don't come back. And if you ever want another job, I'll make good and sure that you don't get it.'

Ross was finished.

When news of Hewitt's return from the dead came over the radio to the sergeant at Ross's house, he drove straight to Kirkbrae to see for himself. He took one look, left the constable to check that nothing untoward had actually happened to Hewitt and drove, with the Chief Superintendent still in tow, to the Brodie camp where Tam, Clunie and Greg were drinking tea.

The sergeant said nothing. He just walked up to the three of them and joined them by the fire, squatted down and warmed his hands. Then he spoke into the flames, as if to himself.

'It's called wasting police time, in this case a lot of time.

110

I've even had to call out a search party which wasn't needed. No proof, of course. Nothing a man could follow up. But, by me, Brodie, this thing is down to you.'

Tam said nothing. There was no need. The sergeant stood up. 'Is it no time, Brodie, that you were maybe shifting?'

'Past time,' said Tam. 'But I'm on a slow fence. Bad ground. Nothing but rock and stanes. I'll be away in twa days, though. Twa days will see me oot.'

'Good, Brodie. Don't make it three.'

The sergeant turned on his heel and went back to the car, accompanied by the Chief Superintendent who had remained silent throughout.

Greg's mother had a fit when she saw the state he was in but believed the hornet story. Clunie's stinging was sufficiently recent in her mind for her not to notice that the crushed insects which fell out when Greg took his shirt off were definitely bees.

Greg knew that the sergeant had only brought forward something that was going to happen anyway. Tam and Clunie would have left Kirkbrae in a few weeks if for no other reason than that their season was drawing to a close. He knew now that in two days they would be gone.

Strangely, the last two days were like so many others, nothing special or final about them. Tam and Clunie were both gone all day at the fence, which had indeed turned difficult, and Greg only saw a little of them in the evenings when he walked the dog. His mother insisted that he stay close to home until the stings went down.

In a way it was better that the last two days were as they were. Why make a song and dance?

On the last evening, they shared a drum round the fire as if it were just another night. But Clunie clasped her

111

knees in her hands and looked a little sad and Tam fussed with the fire in a way that wasn't like him. Greg had no doubt that after tonight things would be different. He didn't altogether like the idea. In fact, he didn't like it at all. 'I'm going to miss you,' he said.

'Aye, son.' said Tam. 'And it's no goin' tae be the same withoot ye. Or that daft big dug,' he said to Dusty.

The time came. One moment there were sitting round the fire all three and the next it was the no-denying hour to say goodbye. Tam and Clunie were better at it than Greg. Perhaps they'd more practice, or were more aware that leave-taking and meeting again are part of the same cycle. Tam shook Greg by the hand and spoke his address with the blessing that he would be welcome. Greg thanked Tam for the summer and meant it.

Clunie didn't shake hands. She saw Greg from the camp to the road. Walked with him through the fir trees to where the water splashed from its pipe. He said goodbye and wanted to say much more.

'We'll find ye,' she said, which was a lovely tinker thing to say and she kissed him.

Next day he stayed away from the camp. He knew they had left with the first light but to visit so soon would have seemed like an intrusion. However, the day after that was different and he was unable to deny himself a visit.

What struck him was the smallness of the place, especially the dry, pressed patch where the tent had been. He looked at the still clear tracks from the van tyres and the stones which held the fire. There was so little left.

Greg went to the fire and with his finger wrote in the ash, 'Clunie Brodie'. He wanted to add, 'The girl from the green and pleasant place', but all there was room for was her name.